The Presence of Grace
Anie Michaels

The Presence of Grace
© *Copyright Anie Michaels 2016*

Edited by Hot Tree Editing.
Cover design © Hang Le byhangle.com

To anyone who has ever lost hope,
keep searching.

Prologue

Grace

Have you ever seen a grown man cry?

I mean, *really* cry? Not the single tear that gets wiped away before anyone sees it. I'm talking about the body-wracking, lung-seizing, shoulder-shaking kind of crying.

I hadn't, not before that night.

Sure, I'd seen a few guys get choked up, but they were usually always drunk and the tears were sports related.

But not that time.

He was hunched over, elbows on his knees, leaning against the brick of the building, face in his hands, and he was sobbing.

I'd just left the school, but he hadn't heard the doors open. They took their sweet time closing thanks to the little gadgets that kept them from slamming shut, so I got a good three-second look at this man crying right in front of me. Three seconds is a really long time when you're witnessing someone have an emotional breakdown. They were the longest and saddest three seconds of my life. Granted, it was dark outside, and he was huddled against the wall, but I could tell he wasn't a small man. He was built. Large. *Manly*. And watching him cry was almost painful. I never could have imagined what would make a man like him sob.

When the door finally closed, the soft thump jarred him and I watched as his head snapped up and he finally noticed me.

I was frozen, stunned really, afraid to move or speak, hoping maybe I could spare us both the embarrassment of the moment. I didn't know if I should continue the short distance to my car, turn around and go back into the building, or acknowledge the crying man.

He stood up fully, raking his hands down his face, which immediately and unconsciously awakened my kindergarten teacher reflexes. I reached into my giant purse and pulled out a few tissues, took the last few steps between us, and held them out.

"Here, take these."

His eyes met mine, then traveled down to my outstretched hand, and he slowly accepted them. He used them to wipe his eyes and nose, then just let his head rest against the wall, taking deep breaths.

"Are you all right? Do you need me to call someone?" My question trailed off at the end. I wasn't sure what I was supposed to do to help this crying, albeit handsome, stranger.

A few moments later, a very deep and raspy voice answered, "No, thank you. There's no one to call."

His answer sounded more painful than factual, as if my even asking him that had opened the wound up further. I had no idea what I was supposed to do next.

"You seem really upset. Do you want to talk about it?" Why did I ask him that? He didn't know me and there was no reason he should want to unload his problems on me, but he was breaking my heart with his tearstained cheeks and breaths that were stuttering in and out while his lungs tried to catch up with his emotions.

His eyes met mine again, bravely, but his face scrunched up and his bottom lip found its way between his teeth. Then he started crying again.

"Oh, shit," I whispered, upset with myself for making him cry. I hurried to his side just as he bent at the waist again, and awkwardly rubbed my hand up and down his back. I'd never known it was possible to feel so uncomfortable and so helpless at the same time. "Please, please don't cry. I'm sorry. I'm sure everything will be just fine." I was grasping at straws, saying every clichéd thing you would think to say to your crying girlfriend when she broke up with her asshole boyfriend, but it didn't seem to work on this man, whose back, I noticed while trying to comfort him, was nothing but firm, taut muscle. Tendons moved in tandem as his breaths pulled in and then rushed back out.

A few minutes passed, long minutes of him crying and me offering him a gentle hand at his back. When he finally stood up, I handed him more tissues and waited for I don't know what.

Eventually he spoke.

"My wife died a few months ago," he murmured, his words both shaky and sad. "This is the first time I've been to parent-teacher conferences without her."

Oh, God.

Oh. *God.*

"I'm so sorry," I say honestly. It was the saddest thing anyone had ever said to me, and with just those few words, the tears started to well in my own eyes. I managed to push them back, to swallow the pinching in my throat. This man might not have needed me, but I felt as though I was supposed to help him, not cry along with him.

"I'm a mess," he whispered, standing at full height again.

"I think you're allowed to be a mess."

We were both silent for another moment, standing against the brick wall, nothing but the sound of night between us, and then he spoke again.

"Every day I think to myself, 'It has to be better today. It can't be any worse than yesterday.' But then something else happens and I realize I'm alone, and that she'll never be here again, and it's like a sledgehammer to the gut."

I wanted to know how she'd died, but I didn't dare ask. I hoped though, for her sake, she hadn't suffered.

"I'm no expert, and I've never dealt with this kind of loss, but I think it does get better eventually." I hated the sound of my words, hated the way they weren't helpful, especially since all this man seemed to need in that moment was help. "What grade is your child in?" I hoped distraction would work.

"Ruby," he said wistfully, and I swore I saw the pain fade from his face for just a moment while a tiny smile turned up the corners of his mouth. "She's in second grade."

"Fun age," I mused.

"You have kids?"

"No," I answered, hating the somber intonation of my voice. I nodded toward the building. "I'm a teacher."

His eyes widened slightly. "You're a teacher… here?"

"Yeah. But don't worry, I don't teach second grade." I laughed, trying to make him feel better, trying to offer a joke to lighten the mood. It must have worked because a moment later he let out a soft laugh.

"I'll let you get back to your evening," he said, straightening up and wiping his hands, damp from his tears, on his thighs.

"Are you sure you're all right? I'm in no hurry, if you need to talk to someone."

"No, I'm honestly really embarrassed you caught me crying to begin with." He let out a real laugh then, and all the muscles in my body that I hadn't realized were tense let out a sigh of relief.

"Don't be too hard on yourself. I'm sure you're doing a great job." He didn't respond, but he did give me a sad smile, so I took that as my cue to leave. I gave him a tiny wave and continued toward the parking lot. I hoped he got his wish and that tomorrow would be better than today.

Three Years Later

Chapter One

Devon

"Ruby, you have ten minutes to be outside waiting for the bus. Jax, you absolutely have to brush your teeth this morning. I never should have let you skip last night."

I said practically the same thing every morning, gave the same warnings and the same countdowns, but it seemed like we were always just seconds away from disaster. Well, disaster in the form of missing the bus. It wouldn't be the worst thing in the world, but it definitely would throw a kink in my plans for the day.

"Dad," Ruby whined as she came into the kitchen where I was packing Jaxy's lunch. "I don't have anything to wear."

"That is statistically impossible. Grandma just took you shopping last weekend." Not to mention I'd just stuffed her drawers full of clothes the night before after an evening of folding laundry.

"I can't find anything I want to wear."

"We passed finding what you *want* to wear twenty minutes ago, Ruby. You need to go put on a top and some jeans. Your bus will be here in"—I looked at the clock on the microwave— "eight minutes." She puffed out an irritated breath and marched back to her bedroom. As soon as she was out of sight, Jaxy waltzed into the kitchen and hopped up on one of the barstools. "You brush your teeth?" I asked, not even bothering to look up. I was good at making lunches, but not blindly.

"Yeah. Did you fill out my book order form?"

"I did last night. It's all in your backpack."

"Did you get me the books I circled?" he asked excitedly. At that point I did look at him. I loved watching my kids getting excited over books. Jaxy, being in second grade, was just getting to the point where he really excelled at reading independently, and books without big, colorful pictures were becoming appealing. Olivia had loved to read and I was so glad both our kids had gotten that from her.

"I got you a *few* of the books you circled, but I supplemented those with a few that I think will challenge you." A smile spread slowly across his face.

"Cool. Thanks, Dad." His lips pulled up to form the exact same smile as his mother. My eyes darted to the large photo of her hanging over the fireplace across the room. The ache was still there, still burned in my chest when I thought about everything Olivia was missing out on, but what gave me hope was that the ache was slowly dulling.

When we'd moved to Florida two and a half years prior, just months after Olivia's death, I'd been a mess. I'd wanted to stay in the town and house we'd raised our children in, thinking it would be best for Ruby and Jax, but I couldn't function there and needed the support of my parents. Moving to Florida had been hard—starting over was not something I'd ever thought I'd have to do—but having my mom and dad so close proved to be invaluable. My kids now had a strong bond with my parents, and I'd had the help I needed from the right people. People who were supposed to hold me up, supposed to love me through the hard times.

My concentration was broken when my phone buzzed in my pocket. I pulled it out and saw Evelyn's name across the screen. Hesitating for more than one reason, I convinced myself that five minutes before the bus was scheduled to pick my kids up wasn't a good time to take a call. I sent her to voice mail and hoped she didn't take it personally.

My phone went back in my pocket and I zipped up Jaxy's lunch box, setting it in front of him on the bar just as Ruby emerged from her room again, this time dressed for school.

"Oh, look. You managed to find some clothes to wear."

"Barely," she mumbled under her breath. The closer Ruby got to preteen, the mouthier she became.

"I think you look nice," I offered sincerely.

"This skirt squeezes my fat belly." Her eyes cast down over her body.

Red flags were flying in my mind. Lately, Ruby had become more and more aware of her body, and I'd known this was coming, but that didn't mean I knew how to handle it. Ruby wasn't overweight, not by a long shot. Honestly, her stomach was the softest part of her, but it wasn't something she needed to worry about.

"Ruby," I said gently as I ran a hand down the back of her hair. "Your belly isn't fat. You're not fat. You're beautiful. If the skirt doesn't fit, we can find something else."

Her eyes slowly met my gaze and she looked sad. "It's okay, Daddy. I don't have any time left." She turned away and locked her gaze on her brother. "Jax, let's go. And don't try to sit next to me on the bus this time."

Jaxy simply walked behind her, mimicking her with a high-pitched, singsong voice. I smiled because little brothers were jerks. I followed them until I got to the threshold of the house, then leaned against the doorjamb, keeping a safe distance. Ruby had informed me earlier in the school year that it wasn't *cool* to have your dad at the bus stop. I told her I wasn't about to let them wait unsupervised, to which she rolled her eyes. We compromised by agreeing I'd wait at the door. Luckily for Ruby, the bus stop was at the end of our driveway.

The bus came, collected my children, and drove away while Jaxy waved at me from the window. Taking one last sip of coffee from my mug, I grabbed my keys and headed out the door.

Before we moved to Florida, I'd had a suit-and-tie job as a business consultant. It had been really good money and that was mainly what kept me there. Raising a family was expensive and Olivia had wanted to be a stay-at-home mom. But in Florida, my priorities changed. I was the only parent they had left and I couldn't spend fourteen hours a day at a desk anymore. When I was ready to go back to work, my dad offered me a position at his hardware store. He'd built a thriving business, and every summer from ages thirteen to eighteen I'd worked for him. He'd always wanted to pass the business down to one of his children, and was more than happy to hire me when I needed a job.

Working for my dad allowed me to leave the house after the kids got on the bus, and to be home in time to make sure they ate dinner and finished their homework. Four days a week the kids were dropped off at a care center until I could go get them after work. Jaxy still liked going there, but Ruby was reaching the age where she definitely didn't think she needed a babysitter. There were a few kids there her age, but not many, and I knew she hated it. I also knew that once she hit sixth grade, I'd have to let her stay home alone after school.

I parked my SUV and walked toward the happy-looking building where I could hear the elated screams of children playing on the playground out back. It wasn't quite spring yet, so the temperature was still cool enough that playing outside was feasible.

I pulled open the door and anticipated the cool rush of air that blasted me in the face. Air-conditioning was no joke here. Approaching the front counter, I tried to keep my head down, not wanting to bring too much attention to myself. But my efforts to remain unseen didn't work—they never did.

"Mr. Roberts." I heard her overly friendly voice coming from the office to my left, then heard the slap of her heels on the linoleum floor. I kept my gaze down on the sign-out sheet. "I was beginning to worry about you. Running a little late today." Candace was, for all intents and purposes, a very nice woman. She was probably just a few years younger than I was, pretty in the I-spend-an-hour-in-front-of-the-mirror-every-morning-to-look-like-this way, and very, *very* persistent. When the kids first started going there, she immediately tried to catch my eye. I wasn't in a good space then, and turned her down, eventually having to straight-out tell her my wife had just died and I wasn't looking to date anyone. She'd obviously taken that as an indication that when I was ready to date, she'd be up first.

"Traffic," I replied evenly, finally bringing my face up and meeting her gaze, giving her a forced smile.

"Jaxy is full of energy today." She laughed. "But that's not different from any other day, I suppose." She crossed her arms and leaned down on the counter, her low-cut shirt falling completely open as a sly grin spread across her face. "I get off in twenty minutes. Maybe we could all go to Joe's Pizza and let the kids play video games while we sit and have some adult conversation."

It had been a while since Candace had asked me out, and I'd hoped she'd gotten the hint, but apparently I was going to have to find new ways to turn her down. "It's a school night, and the kids still need to do their homework." I gave her another forced smile and entered the security code on a number pad that opened the gate to the part of the facility where the kids were.

"Pity," she said with an exaggerated pout forming on her lips. "Maybe some other time."

I didn't answer, just kept walking, hoping she'd think I hadn't heard the last part. I wasn't accustomed to telling women I didn't want to date them. Candace was pushy, but she didn't mean any harm. One day, I'd have to just tell her, straight out, I wasn't interested in her.

"Dad!" Jaxy saw me through a window and ran inside, greeting me with a big hug. Ruby wandered in slowly, but still managed a halfhearted side hug. I'd take it. I'd take any show of affection from my moody preteen.

"You guys ready to go home?" I asked, my arms still wrapped around them.

"Yeah," Jaxy said.

"Definitely," Ruby added.

I laughed.

"Let's go then."

"Okay, kids. Homework time," I said as I placed the dinner dishes in the sink. It had been spaghetti night. I wasn't a master chef, but there were a few dishes I managed without burning the house down that tasted decent. They were on a weekly rotation and when the kids got tired of the same seven meals, I tried to throw something in to surprise them. The surprises only worked out about 50 percent of the time. The other 50 percent were pizza nights after my failed attempts ended up in the trash.

Schoolwork was one area where both the kids excelled. Rarely did I ever have to get after them to do their homework, and I enjoyed helping them if they needed it. They each grabbed their backpacks, took a stool at the bar, and made themselves comfortable. As I did every evening at homework time, I poured them each a glass of chocolate milk. In about a half hour, I'd pop some popcorn and let them munch on it as they worked.

"What do we have going on this evening?" I asked as I set the glasses down in front of them, flinging a kitchen towel over my shoulder.

"I have to read this story about the Oregon Trail and then write a paragraph about it," Ruby said, holding up a small book.

"I can sum up the Oregon Trail in two words: wagons and dysentery."

"What's dis-sin-tury?" Jaxy asked, slowly pronouncing the unfamiliar word.

"It means they pooped themselves to death." Both kids immediately broke into fits of giggles and I leaned back, watching my children laugh. Even if it was at the word poop, I could listen to them laugh forever. When the laughter died off, and it took a few minutes, I asked Jaxy, "What about you? What are you working on this evening?"

"I have a math packet," he replied, opening his backpack. "Oh, and Miss Richards sent home this letter."

My gut immediately dropped. Letters from teachers were notoriously bad things. My mind buzzed with what Jax could have done and how much trouble he might be in.

"What'd you do?" I asked, my tone indicating I believed him already guilty.

"Nothing, I swear! I was just sitting at my desk and Miss Richards told me there's a letter in my bag for you. I didn't get into any trouble." He shoved the envelope at me like it was proof of his innocence.

I took it from him with a skeptical look, but proceeded to open it.

Dear Mr. Roberts,

It is with great excitement that I write to inform you of Jax's invitation to join the Talented and Gifted Program at North Elm Elementary. Jax has always been a bright student, so I am not surprised he has earned this honor. I would like to discuss plans with you at a parent/teacher conference. Please e-mail me to discuss possible meeting times.

Jax is a pleasure to have in class and I can't wait to help him with this next big step in his education.

Best Regards,
Miss Richards
2nd Grade Teacher
North Elm Elementary
g.richards@nee.com

I read the letter once, and then I read it again. I looked up to Jaxy, who had started his math worksheet, obviously not caring too much about what the letter said.

"Jaxy, this letter says you got into TAG."

"What's TAG?"

"TAG is an acronym for talented and gifted."

"What's an acronym?" he asked, faced scrunched up.

"It's when they use the first letters of words to make a new word. Kind of like a shortcut," I answered with a laugh.

"Oh," he said slowly. I could picture the wheels turning in his brain. "Cool. Can we have popcorn now?"

Chapter Two

Devon

Getting my mom to watch my kids was not difficult. She loved having them. My dad did too, but we all knew what was up. Grandma was in charge and she made the plans for the grandkids. Dad was just along for the ride, and he enjoyed them just as much as she did. It was a bonus, however, when I asked if they could take the kids on a Friday night and my mom suggested a sleepover.

I love my kids just as much as the next dad, but a night off from parenting and a Saturday morning to sleep in? You couldn't ask for more than that. I dropped them off with their overnight bags, and they couldn't even be bothered to give me a good-bye hug before they ran off into the wonderland that was their grandparents' house.

"I'll be by tomorrow by eleven to pick them up," I said to my mother as I handed the bags over to her. My parents started having kids early, but I was the youngest so by the time they'd had me they were close to thirty. I worried sometimes that overnight visits were too much for them. I wanted them to enjoy the kids, but not to the detriment of their health. "You can call me if you have any problems and I'll come back to get them. All I have planned is this parent/teacher conference."

"There won't be a problem," my mother responded, looking at me like I might have offended her. "I raised five kids. I know how to handle little ones."

"Of course, Mom. I didn't mean any harm."

"I know, baby," she said, leaning over the threshold and pressing a kiss against my cheek. "Go. Be kid free for an evening."

"All right. I'll see you tomorrow." She shut the door before I was even done speaking. "All right then," I said to myself. I turned and walked back down the driveway and got into my car.

When I arrived at North Elm Elementary, I noticed the parking lot was empty aside from one or two cars. I figured Friday evenings weren't the most popular time to be at a school. The front doors were still unlocked and I followed the instructions from Miss Richards's e-mail to her classroom. The halls were empty too, and I couldn't help but feel as though I was somewhere I wasn't supposed to be. The lights were dimmed and my footsteps echoed through the halls. An empty school was weirdly creepy.

I found the door with Jaxy's teacher's name above, knocked lightly, and then pushed the door open slightly.

"Miss Richards?" I called out softly.

"Yes, please, come in," a soft feminine voice replied. I pushed the door open, but didn't see anyone. I took a step in, my eyes sweeping the room, and a brunette woman appeared from around the corner. She was looking down at the papers in her hand, but when she finally glanced up at me, she halted.

My eyes narrowed at her and my brain started running a thousand miles an hour, trying desperately to figure out why she looked so familiar.

She took the last two steps to me, her hand held out, but had an utterly confused look on her face that more than likely matched mine.

"Grace Richards," she said slowly as I took her hand.

"Have we met—"

"Do I know you—"

We both spoke at the same time, our hands wrapped around each other's.

"You look really familiar," I said slowly, moving our hands up and down even more slowly.

"Did you come to the parent/teacher conferences at the beginning of the year?" she asked.

"No," I replied, shaking my head. "My mother came in my place."

Our hands were still joined, and we were still staring each other down, unable or unwilling to move past the weird sensation that we were obviously both having. After a few more moments of thoughtful silence and slow hand shaking, her mouth formed into a perfect O and her free hand came up to cover it.

"Oh my gosh," she said, gently pulling her hand from mine.

"What?" This was the strangest meeting I'd ever had.

"You're the crying man."

"The crying man?" I asked, pulling back in confusion.

"Back in Fairbanks. At Ridgefield Elementary. I was a teacher there. And you were the man crying outside during parent/teacher conferences."

It took a moment or two to remember, but finally the puzzle piece fell into place. It was her. The poor woman who'd happened upon me as I had a nervous breakdown outside of Ruby's second grade conferences. Olivia had only been gone a few months and I'd thought I could handle going alone, but I hadn't been prepared to see all the mothers and fathers there with each other, all the couples and partners spending an evening together. It hadn't occurred to me it would even be an issue. I hadn't even made it to Ruby's classroom before I lost my composure.

"You were there," she continued, "and I felt so helpless because there wasn't anything to say or do."

Embarrassed, I ran my hand through my hair, trying to find the words. Any words. "Wow," I finally managed. "This is awkward." I gave a small laugh, trying to cover the fact that I felt very uncomfortable.

"No, no, no," she insisted. "I'm really glad to see you. I think about you all the time."

"You do?"

"Yeah. I think often about how you're doing. You were so upset that night."

"It wasn't my best moment."

Her eyebrows shot up as if she'd just came to another realization. "You're Jax's dad."

"Devon Roberts. Nice to meet you."

"Wow," she whispered. "It really is a small world."

"Yeah," I agreed with a laugh, unsure of where to go from there.

"Okay, so your son, Jax," she said, moving the conversation along. "He's a wonderful kid." She led me to a long table at the front of her room. She took a seat on one side and motioned for me to sit across from her. "He's a pleasure to have in class. Super attentive. Always eager to learn. Just a great kid. A great student."

"Uh, thanks. That's good to hear."

She smiled and it caught my attention. It wasn't the polite smile she'd forced when I'd first arrived, and it wasn't the worried smile she'd given me when we'd realized how we'd previously met. It was a genuine smile. Soft and warm. It lit up her entire face, all the way to her eyes. I wasn't sure if I'd ever noticed a brunette with blue eyes before—I must have known at least one—but her eyes were almost the color of the sky on a clear summer day. Deeply blue. She was radiant and the smile was reflective of that.

She pulled some papers from a folder and spread them out in front of me.

"These are the tests Jax took at the beginning of the year. We give these tests to gauge a baseline for all the students, so we can measure progress. As you can see, he scored high, well above his classmates." She pulled out even more papers and laid them out the same way. "These are his test scores from earlier this month. As you can see," she said, using her hands to delicately point out his scores, "his scores are now leaps and bounds above his grade level."

"That's great," I replied. I was out of my element.

"It *is* great. But he's not just smart. You see, the difference between a bright student and a talented and gifted student is very clear. Jax doesn't just like learning, he isn't doing his work because we ask him to, he *loves* learning. He seeks out knowledge and asks questions the other students, even the best of students, don't think about asking."

"He's always been very inquisitive."

"Yes!" she exclaimed, her face brightening even more—something I wouldn't have thought possible if I hadn't witnessed it myself. "He's constantly asking questions, always wanting to know more. I can't tell you how many times I've had to pull out my phone to look up the answers to questions he has. It's incredible." She took a breath, still smiling, and then pulled out another paper. "So, here's the information on TAG. Right now, our school is offering a TAG class once a week after school on Fridays. We're also planning for a field trip closer to the end of the year— somewhere educational like the zoo or the aquarium. There's no cost to you. We're required by law to offer specialized education to all students who demonstrate a need."

"And the class is taught by a teacher at this school?"

"Oh, gosh, I should have mentioned—I am the TAG director here. So it's taught by me."

"So, basically, what you're saying is that Jaxy gets to stay after school on Fridays and take an extra class with other high-performing students?"

"That's *exactly* what I'm saying." She smiled again, and this time it was contagious. I smiled back.

"Sounds like a no-brainer. Oh, except for transportation. Jaxy and his sister ride the bus to day care after school on Fridays."

"Oh, yes, Ruby. Jax talks about her a lot. He thinks she's the best." A little bit of warmth spread through me at her words. "Transportation isn't an issue. We're required to provide that as well. A bus will just take him to day care when we're done, or the bus can take him home, or you can even pick him up. Whatever works for you." She pulled another stack of papers from her folder and slid it over to me. "This is the admission form, and it spells everything out for you. You just fill it out and send it back to school with Jax, and he'll be all set to go."

"It's strange hearing someone call him Jax," I said absently as I flipped through the papers.

"Oh?"

"We always call him Jaxy." Her eyes went soft when I told her the nickname.

"That's sweet. He's a really special boy."

"I agree."

"Well," she said, letting out a sigh, "that's all the info I have for you. I don't want to keep you from your Friday night plans."

I let out a laugh. "My parents took the kids overnight, and my plans included this meeting. Now all that's waiting for me is a quiet, empty house." I said the words with more sadness than I anticipated. I was looking forward to having a night alone, but I hadn't anticipated being lonely.

"We've got that in common," she said with a smile as she scooped up all the papers she'd laid out for me.

Before I could even think about filtering the words, they tumbled out of my mouth. "Can I take you for a cup of coffee?" Her hands stilled, her fingers still grasping the papers, and her eyes met mine. "Not, like, a date," I hurriedly stuttered, "just like a thank you coffee for crying all over you last time we met."

"I don't know," she said slowly, a worried look in her eyes.

"No, you're right. It's a bad idea." I stood up and, taking my packet of papers with me, moved toward the door. "It was nice meeting you… um… again." I threw up a hasty wave, but just before I made it to the door, she stopped me.

"Wait," she called, her voice still sounding unsure. "There's a great little bistro on Fifth Street downtown called Marco's. They're open late on Fridays. I was going to go there after work and grade some papers, maybe grab a sandwich. I'll be there for the next few hours."

"You won't mind a little distraction?" I asked, hoping she wouldn't.

"Are you kidding? I talk to seven-year-olds all day. I would love to talk to an adult about something normal for a little while." She smiled again and all my nerves dissipated. I didn't know why I was nervous. It wasn't like I'd asked her on a date. We were just two adults who didn't have any plans and decided to grab something to eat.

"Okay, I'll see you there in a little while." I waved again, this time a little less rabidly, and left. I made it into the hall and around the corner before I let out the breath I'd been holding. I ran a hand through my hair and kept walking. It had been a very long time since I'd been alone with a woman. I hadn't even thought about whether or not I was ready to take this step before I'd blurted out the words.

My thoughts immediately went to Olivia, and even though it was ridiculous, I felt guilty for planning to meet with a woman. And as if my guiltometer needed to be calibrated, my phone rang in my pocket. It turned out to be Evelyn calling. I'd dodged her phone call earlier in the week and couldn't bring myself to ignore her again. She didn't deserve that.

"Hey, Evie," I answered, trying to sound upbeat.

"Devon, hi. How are you?"

"Good. Just leaving a conference with Jaxy's teacher."

"Oh, yeah? Are the kids there?"

"No, they're with my mom."

"Oh." She sounded disappointed. "But that's probably good. Do you have a second?"

"Yeah, sure," I replied, pushing the doors of the school open and walking out into the warm air of the night. The tone of Evie's voice worried me though; she sounded like she had bad news. Or news she thought I wouldn't take well.

Evie and I had been on better terms since she'd come to visit us a few months before. There'd been a period when we didn't really communicate. I let her talk to the kids whenever she wanted, encouraged it even. Evie was one of the last connections Ruby and Jaxy had to their mother and I would never keep her away, but it was too difficult to talk to her myself. But a lot of good had come of her visit. Seeing her happy and healthy went a long way to making me feel like we'd all made the right decisions, like we'd actually done what was best for everyone.

"Nate and I want to fly to Florida during the kids' spring break and take them to Disney World." Evie pushed the words out rapidly and I knew she was nervous. I could tell by the tone of her voice she had her eyes squeezed shut and her cheeks bunched up, bracing for the worst. I could picture her in my head. "We don't want to intrude, so if you already have plans, I completely understand. I just miss them and thought it would be something fun—"

"Evie, slow down. Breathe." I heard her give a sad and nervous laugh, but then she inhaled and exhaled, loud enough for me to hear her. "Okay, so you're coming to Florida and you want to go to Disney World?"

"We thought it would be fun. Have they been yet?"

"Yeah, but it was almost two years ago and I mean, come on, it's Disney." The air in my SUV was stifling. Even after almost three years I hadn't learned to crack my windows. I started the car and cranked the air-conditioning.

"So you wouldn't mind if we came for a visit?"

"Of course not." I heard a girly squeal and could picture Evie bouncing up and down, her blonde ponytail swinging behind her. It had taken a while for the ache to go away every time I thought about her, so I was glad when picturing her didn't make me uncomfortable. Quite the opposite, in fact. Hearing Evie happy made me happy. We could add that to the list of things we never thought would happen: perhaps I'd managed to release the weird hold I'd had on Evie since we were in college. But then again, I never actually had her to begin with.

Chapter Three

Grace

"You've made a terrible mistake," I said to myself, turning my car into a spot at Marco's. I'd been telling myself variations of that same sentiment the entire drive there. "Nothing good can come of this," I mumbled, putting the car in park and pulling the keys from the ignition.

He'd looked almost exactly as I remembered him, which was surprising seeing as how the last time I saw him he was standing in the dark, crying. His hair was blond. He was tall and broad. Well-built. Big, but not overly bulky. Back in Fairbanks he'd been wearing a light jacket when I found him crying against the wall of the school, but tonight he'd just been wearing a polo shirt. My eyes had immediately been drawn to the way his sleeves stretched across his biceps, which were large and defined.

"Oh, my goodness. This is a terrible idea." I let my forehead rest against the steering wheel, trying to give my thoughts an opportunity to settle. I couldn't *not* go in. He was a parent. He'd think I was rude. But he was *a parent*. Certainly I couldn't meet a parent at a bistro on a Friday night, for no academic purpose. This had to be against all kinds of rules.

But even though there were a million reasons not to go in, I still felt compelled. There was something about him that pulled at me. There was this strange need to make sure he was all right. After three years of thinking about him, I couldn't pass up an opportunity to talk to him.

It was with that small goal I opened my car door and climbed out, making my way to the bistro.

Mr. Roberts was standing just inside the doors, hands in his pockets. He turned to me as I walked in, and smiled. For just one moment I was breathless. He was truly beautiful. Without my permission, my lips tipped up and smiled in response.

"I was afraid you wouldn't show," he said quietly as I approached.

"That would be rude."

"But understandable. This probably isn't technically allowed." His smile turned sheepish as he shrugged.

I didn't respond because I didn't really know what to say. He was right. This wasn't allowed. But, as far as I was concerned, it was completely innocent.

Mostly innocent.

"There's a great spot in the back. They'll bring us a menu." I waved a hand and indicated I wanted him to follow me. Luckily, my favorite table was available. This was a great spot, but it wasn't exactly a happening place. On a Friday evening there were a lot more exciting places for people to be.

Just as I'd said, as soon as we were seated a waiter brought us both water and a menu.

"This is a nice place," Mr. Roberts said, looking around.

"I come here most Fridays. They're really friendly and let me sit here for hours. In fact, they're probably wondering what I'm doing here with another person. I've always been alone." I said the words and then felt the stinging in my gut. I hadn't *always* been alone, but the sentence made me feel empty anyhow. "I mean, I've never come here with another person."

"The idea of going to a restaurant alone seems both terrifying and wonderful." He smiled again.

"It's peaceful, that's for sure. But it's lonely sometimes," I said honestly. Being lonely wasn't the worst thing a person could be.

He was quiet for a moment as he looked over his menu, but then said softly, "It's funny, because my idea of lonely is probably very different than yours. Or most people's, for that matter."

I took his words as a sort of invitation to talk about what was on my mind. "How've you been? You know, since I saw you last?" He exhaled loudly and I realized he might not want to talk about it. "I'm sorry, I don't mean to pry, but I wasn't lying when I said I think about you all the time. I wonder about you." I lift one shoulder in a shrug. "You were really upset."

"I should have never tried to go that night. It was a bad decision." He ran a hand through his blond hair and I watched it fall right back into place. "Olivia had only been gone a short while. I hadn't anticipated how it would feel to see married couples, parents, at an event like that. It just kind of struck a nerve, you could say."

"Wow," I said wistfully. "I can't even imagine."

"You were very gracious that night," he said as his eyes met mine.

"All I did was hand you a few Kleenex."

"Yeah, but you could have just kept walking. You could have ignored me."

"You would have been fine."

"Probably, but you didn't know that. Not everyone would stop to help a perfect stranger."

His praise was making me uncomfortable, displayed by the blush on my cheeks. "And what are the odds that you and I both end up in Florida three years later? Meeting at another elementary school?"

28 | The Presence of Grace

"It is peculiar, isn't it?" he said, smiling again. He clasped his hands and rested his elbows on the table, peering at me over his hands. "My parents have lived here my whole life. After Olivia died, just a little while after my breakdown at the parent-teacher conferences, I decided to move back home to be close to them, so they could help with the kids."

"It's great that you have that kind of support system."

"Yes, but why are you here?"

I brought my water glass to my mouth, sipping slowly, trying to find the right words. "Things in Fairbanks didn't work out. I'd spent a summer here once when I was younger." I shrugged, trying to seem nonchalant. "I figured it was a good place to start over."

"I found you. I foiled your plan," he stated with a straight face.

"No," I said, laughing softly. "My plan was foiled long before you came around."

The waiter returned to take our order, then left us in peace once more.

"So, there's you and the kids, and your parents. Anyone else?" I hated the way I sounded, as if I was fishing for information. I totally was, but I wanted to sound less obvious about it. Fortunately, he continued providing information I wasn't entitled to, without sounding put out by it.

"I have brothers and sisters, but they're spread out all over the country. It's all right, though. The kids and I pretty much have it all figured out by now. My parents help a lot, but they don't really see it as helping. They see it as just spending time with their grandkids."

"That's good," I replied. I had one more question burning through me, and it was the worst one I could think of asking, but something about Devon's open nature and calm demeanor made me feel as though he would tell me anything. "Can I ask how she died?"

"Breast cancer," he said almost immediately, the words cold, as if he were trying so hard to say them without emotion. As if he were holding himself back from spitting them.

"I'm sorry. That must have been so hard." I'd never been close to anyone who passed from cancer, but I knew it wasn't a quick and painless road.

"It was. But," he continued on a sigh, "we've made it through the hardest parts. We'll persevere." We both paused and I had no idea where to go from there. Luckily, he kept talking. "I couldn't help but notice there's no ring on your finger. But there is a tan line."

I looked down at my ring finger before I could stop myself. Sure enough, the line was still there. It had taken a while for the indentation to go away, but finally it had. My thumb rubbed over the spot where my wedding ring used to be.

"My husband and I split up about two and a half years ago."

"I'm sorry."

"I'm not." That was a lie. "Okay, I'm a little sorry," I stated.

"Kids?" he asked innocently.

"No," I replied, trying not to let the black sludge I felt swirling around inside me seep out with my words.

"I'm not sure whether that's supposed to be a good thing or not. Kids and divorce is kind of rough. But kids are pretty awesome."

Oh, God.

"Try a room full of thirty of them," I said, forcing a smile on my face, trying desperately to move our conversation back to safe territory. Back to a place that didn't make me want to drown myself.

"Did you always want to teach elementary school?"

And just like that we were safe on dry land.

We talked pleasantly throughout our meal. A few times he laughed and I held my breath, waiting for the wings of the butterflies in my stomach to stop swirling, for my heart to slow to a normal pace. Toward the end of our time together, I let myself study his face. He was pretty magnificent, and I figured it wouldn't hurt to just take the memory of him with me. The first man I'd met who seemed to, perhaps, have more baggage than me, but still seemed to be doing fine. Seemed to be making it through with the scars to prove it, but the life to also prove there were reasons to keep going.

After we'd finished, he walked me to my car. "Thank you for keeping me company, Mr. Roberts," I said as I pulled my keys from my purse.

"Please, call me Devon."

"Only if you promise to call me Grace."

"Deal," he said with a smile that made my breath catch.

"Well," I said, opening my door. "I should probably get going. Thanks again for the company."

"My pleasure. I'll send that packet to school with Jaxy on Monday."

"Sounds good."

"See you around, Grace." He gave a little wave and stepped back onto the sidewalk, watching me settle into my car. I waved back as I drove away, and let out a big sigh. It had been surprisingly comfortable to share a meal with him and I hadn't anticipated that. I hadn't eaten a meal with a man besides family or my ex-husband in years, but Devon made everything seem light and easy.

Nothing in my world had been easy for years.

Chapter Four

Devon

"Have you ever painted your own house?"

I'd been helping an elderly man with supplies to paint his house for over a half hour. He seemed determined, but seeing as how he was making his way through the store with a cane, I had to wonder about his ability.

"No, I can't say that I have. And honestly, I don't know that I would. It's hard work." I watched the old man's face carefully as I said the words, hoping they'd sink in.

"All our kids are grown and moved across the country. I'd tell 'em to come help, but it wouldn't do any good."

I pictured myself old and alone. Would Jaxy and Ruby stay close or run away as far as they could, leaving me to waste away by myself?

"I have the cards of some pretty reputable painting companies up at the register. They hire college kids so the costs are pretty reasonable." I knew if he decided to hire someone else to paint his house I would lose the sale, but I couldn't, in good conscience, send an old man to paint his own house in the Florida sun that was only getting hotter by the day. The man grumbled under his breath for a few seconds, then let out an audible sigh.

"I'm painting the house because I have to sell it. My wife died a year ago and it's just too hard to be there anymore."

Oh, I hear you.

"I'm sorry."

"The point is, I'm painting the house because I want to sell it. I'm starting to think that if I paint it myself, it might not help my cause. I should probably hire a professional."

I laid a gentle hand on his shoulder. "A good paint job can add a lot of value."

"There's no amount of money that can buy the memories of my wife in that house," he said gruffly. "But I can't stay there forever."

"Let me get you those cards." I walked away before he said any more stupidly poignant and emotionally draining things, and headed toward the register. I'd opened the drawer below the register and grabbed a few business cards, when my phone on the counter caught my eye. The light in the corner was flashing. I activated the screen and saw I had five missed calls. Confusion and panic coursed through me. I opened my voice mail and immediately pressed Play.

"Mr. Roberts, this is Amy from Tree Hill Day Care. I'm just calling to let you know that Jaxy hasn't arrived yet, even though we expected him a little while ago. I haven't heard from the school, so I'm not sure if there was a miscommunication or not, but we're still expecting him. Please give us a call so we know you got this message."

"Shit," I swore as I moved on to the next message.

"Um, hi, Devon? Or, uh, Mr. Roberts? This is Miss Richards from North Elm Elementary. I've got Jax here. He's fine and safe, but the bus that usually takes him to day care broke down on the way here. I'm still here with him, so don't worry about that, but I just wanted to let you know. They don't have an estimate of when or if they'll be able to come get him, but I'm here with him and I'll wait to hear from you. Uh, thanks." I heard some rustling, then her voice again. "Oh, and this is my cell phone in case you're confused by the caller ID. You can call me back here, or the school number. Either way. We're on the playground, which is why I called on my cell. Someone will answer if you call the school. Uh, okay. I'll shut up now."

The voice mail ended and I was a mixture of amused and relieved. Grace's message made me chuckle and I was glad she had Jax and he wasn't missing and scared somewhere on a broken-down bus.

"Dad," I hollered to the back of the store, where my father was in the office.

"Yeah?"

"I gotta go pick Jaxy up from school."

I walked back to the old man by the paint samples. "Here you go. I've heard great things about all these companies." I handed him the cards and gave him a gentle clap on the back. "Good luck."

"Thank you," he mumbled, then made his way out of the store.

"Dad," I repeated, sticking my head inside the office. "I gotta go."

"I heard," he said grumpily. "Why didn't the bus pick him up like usual?"

"Broke down,"

"Stuff like this wouldn't happen if you'd just let your mother pick them up and take care of them like she wants."

I rolled my eyes and took in a deep breath. "You and Mom both did your time. You're grandparents, not parents. She shouldn't be picking them up and taking care of them five days a week. She should be spoiling them on Saturday afternoons and watching dance recitals. You guys already do too much."

"One of these days you'll realize that being a parent never ends. Taking care of those kids is no different than taking care of you."

This was an unusually sentimental moment from my father.

"Dad, I gotta go."

"Go, then." He waved a hand at me as if I was annoying him. He was getting grumpy in his old age.

When I arrived at the school I found Jaxy and Grace sitting in the shade of the tree in the front of the building. They were on a blanket with what looked like crackers, juice boxes, and a pile of books.

"Daddy!" Jaxy jumped up and ran toward me, wrapping his arms around me in a running hug.

"Hey, bud. How are you?" I clasped his face in my hands and looked into his eyes.

"I'm fine. Miss Richards has been hanging out with me since my bus didn't show up." I looked up to see Grace folding the blanket they'd just been sitting on. "She gave me a snack and let me read the books only fifth graders are allowed to check out from the library."

"That sounds fun." I let go of his face and took his hand in mine. "Let's go help her pick up." As we approached, Grace caught my eye and a smile spread over her face. She looked happy and something about seeing the smile light her up tugged at me.

"I'm so sorry," I said as I approached.

She waved me away. "Don't worry. It's not a big deal. Stuff happens. It was fun to spend a little one-on-one time with Jax." She winked at him and he giggled.

"Let us help you," I said, reaching for the blanket in her hands.

"Thank you," she said, her voice softer.

Jaxy grabbed the snack garbage and I had the blanket and books. "Lead the way," I said, nodding toward the doors to the school. She turned and started walking, falling into step right next to me. She swiped her key card in front of the sensor and I heard the doors click. Balancing the blanket and books in one hand, I reached forward and opened the door for her. Unfortunately, and much to my embarrassment, Jaxy ran in first.

"Jax," I said firmly, but with a smile, "You always let girls go through doors first. You know that." I turned to Grace, "I'm sorry. Please," I nodded toward the door again. "After you." Her head dipped low and I could have sworn a blush crept over her cheeks.

"Why?" Jax questioned when we were all inside.

"Why, what?" I asked, still a little distracted by the color of Grace's cheeks.

"Why do girls get to go first?"

"Girls and women are precious, Jax. You have to protect them and treat them carefully. That means making sure they go first."

I could see him thinking hard about what I was saying, and finally he spoke. "Ruby can open a door just as good as I can."

I dropped a hand on his shoulder and knelt down in front of him, placing the blanket and books on the floor next to me. "I don't hold the door open for women because I think they can't. I hold doors for women because I respect them and they deserve to be treated well, Jax. Miss Richards deserves your respect, son. All women deserve your respect, but especially Miss Richards. So next time, you let her go first. All right?"

"Okay," he agreed quietly.

"Okay." I let him go with a ruffle of his hair, which made him groan. I picked everything up off the floor and took back up beside Grace. "Sorry about that," I said.

"Don't be," she said softly. We walked quietly next to each other while Jax ran ahead, leading the way.

"They go here," Jax said, pointing to a bookshelf. I held the books out to him one by one and watched as he found their spots, examining each book carefully to determine its place.

"Okay, kid, lead the way to the classroom." Jax ran ahead again and I chuckled.

"Most kids his age would have just put the books anywhere on the shelf. Did you see him organizing the books by author? Alphabetically? It's not typical of a second grader."

"He's always been really detailed," I say casually. I hadn't ever really thought about why Jaxy was the way he was.

"It's just another one of those things that makes him special."

We walked Grace to her classroom and I watched as she placed the blanket in the bottom drawer of a filing cabinet. "Can we walk you out to your car?" I asked, not feeling comfortable leaving her in an almost abandoned building on a Friday evening. The lights throughout the building had been turned off, with only a few left on for necessity.

"Oh, that's not necessary. I have just a few things to finish up before I head home for the weekend. The last thing I want to have to do is come back from spring break with work waiting for me," she said, laughing lightly.

"Wanna know what we're doing this weekend?" Jaxy asked her.

"What?"

"We're going to Disney World!"

"No, way," she exclaimed, matching his enthusiasm. "I've always wanted to go there."

"You haven't gone? Why not? It's only, like, an hour from here."

She shrugged. "Disney isn't really a place you go alone. I'll go someday."

"You could come with us! Auntie Evie and Uncle Nate are coming. Daddy too. You wouldn't be by yourself if you came with us."

She laughed. "That's really sweet, Jax, but you don't need your teacher coming with you to Disney."

"Dad? Can't she come with us?"

I shrugged. "Sure." I smiled at her, knowing I wasn't making it easy for her to refuse. But the truth was, I didn't want her to refuse. For a variety of reasons. The idea of spending an entire day with Evie and Nate was a little overwhelming; I wasn't particularly looking forward to being the third wheel all day. But also, even more so, I wanted to spend time with Grace. More than I'd wanted to spend time with any other woman since Olivia. I wasn't 100 percent sure of how I felt about Grace, but it wasn't just friendly and it wasn't the way I'd felt about his first grade teacher, Mrs. Walden.

I liked Grace. I liked the way she looked, the way she moved, and I liked the way she smiled at my son under the shade of a tree. She was *good*. I could feel it.

"Devon," she whispered, shooting me an annoyed yet amused look. I shrugged again.

"Come to Disney with us. It'll be fun." She looked completely conflicted, which made me happy. She *wanted* to come with us, but obviously didn't think it was appropriate. I selfishly didn't care whether or not it was appropriate. I just wanted to spend more time with her. "If it makes you feel better, you can drive yourself, pay for your own ticket, and just happen to run into us at the entrance at 9:00 a.m."

Her eyes were locked on mine, a smile playing on her lips, and she finally said, "I'll see you at nine."

"Yay! Miss Richards is coming to Disney!"

We both laughed at his excitement.

"You'll be okay here by yourself?" I asked her, catching her gaze again.

"Yeah," she answered softly. I wanted to press the issue, but I decided to let it go and trust she'd be all right.

"Okay. We'll see you in the morning."

"See you then." She gave a little wave. "See you later, Jax. Thanks for keeping me company today."

"It was fun," he said, then ran out of the room as he waved.

"Bye," I said, giving her a nod.

"Bye," she said, smiling.

I turned and walked out of her classroom, thinking how glad I was that bus broke down.

Chapter Five

Grace

I was used to walking through the school building with only the evening lights. I wasn't always the last person to leave, but I'd spent more late nights at school than I cared to admit. It was easy to get lost in lesson planning and grading when there was nothing to go home to. I wasn't afraid to walk to my car alone, but I was more than happy to accept the phone call from my best friend just as I left my classroom.

"Do you know what it reminds me of when you call me just as I'm about to walk through a dark parking lot by myself?" I use as my greeting, knowing Shelby was on the other end of my call. She responds with a laugh. "It reminds me of all the times in college I stupidly walked home from a party by myself and would call you to keep me company."

"Right." Shelby laughed again. "As if being on the phone with someone would stop a murderer from attacking. We were pretty dumb."

"Hey, speak for yourself. I made it through college just fine."

"Why are you walking through a dark parking lot alone? Late night?"

"Yeah. This time it wasn't all my fault though."

"Oh, no?"

"No. A student in my TAG program was stranded here, so I stayed with him until his father came to pick him up."

"You have more patience than me. Hanging out with rug rats isn't my bag."

"That's why your job is so perfect for you. You sit people in chairs and tell them to close their mouths and their eyes while you do their makeup. Then you just get to talk at them while you make them beautiful."

She laughed again, just like I knew she would. Shelby had been my best friend since eighth grade. At eighteen we went to different colleges, but we stayed close even with the distance between us. She'd been there for me through everything and I wasn't sure what I'd ever do without her.

"So, got any plans for the weekend? Isn't it spring break for you now?"

"Yes, spring break officially starts now."

"Gonna go take advantage of all those beautiful beaches?"

"Ugh," I groaned, pushing the doors to the building open and walking out into the air that had cooled slightly since Devon and Jax left. "Spring break is the worst time to go to the beaches in Florida." Then it occurred to me where I was headed tomorrow. "Oh, gosh." I sighed, hitching my purse higher up on my shoulder while still holding the phone to my ear.

"What?" Shelby asked, concerned.

"I got invited to go to Disney World tomorrow. If there's one place worse than the beaches during a school break, it's Disney."

"Who invited you to Disney? That's kind of a weird place to invite a grown-ass woman."

"A man with children."

"A man? With children?" Her interest in my spring break activities was suddenly heightened. "Are you going on a date?"

"No, it's not a date," I insisted. "We're meeting there. I'm buying my own ticket."

"I'm confused. You're going to Disney World with a man and his children, but it's *not* a date?"

"Hold on a sec," I said in a hushed voice. I was just steps from my car, and even though I was sure there was no one around, I still wanted to be careful. Opening the door, I gently tossed my purse on the passenger seat and then folded myself in the car. "The student I stayed late with, he invited me to go along with him and his dad and sister."

"So?"

"So? What do you mean 'so'?"

"I mean, a *student* invites you to Disney World and you politely decline. You pacify him by saying something nice like, 'Oh, maybe next time,' and then he forgets about it. You don't *agree* to go. So, there has to be something else going on here. Is his dad hot?"

Yes.

"That's a ridiculous question," I said sharply, shoving the key in the ignition and cranking the engine.

"So, that's a yes then." I could hear her smiling.

"Okay," I said, pressing the speakerphone button and tossing my phone in the console. "His dad isn't bad looking. And he's a nice guy. But it isn't a date. It's more of a friend thing. Some of his friends are going and I think he wanted to even the numbers a little."

"Another couple? So you're going on a double date to Disney World with a student's parent? You've officially crossed the line from prudish grade school teacher to sexy schoolmarm."

I wanted to explain to Shelby. Wanted to tell her all about how I'd found Devon broken three years ago, how we'd crossed paths in the strangest of coincidences. How, even though I knew he was trying to move on from something completely heartbreaking, there was a not-so-small part of me that felt I could help him through it. It wasn't necessarily attraction I felt toward him, but it wasn't just strictly friendly either. He was the only other person in the world I'd encountered who I felt might feel just as lost as I did. There was some strange sense of solidarity there. I'd felt broken for so long, and I'd begun to think I was alone in my state of fracture. So even though I knew he should have been off-limits, that I should cut ties and just do my job, I couldn't bring myself to snip those tethers I felt holding us together. If nothing else, he could be a friend.

"There's nothing sexy about it, Shelby. He's just a guy with some really great kids and I'm just meeting them at Disney World."

"We'll see," she sang into the phone.

The next morning, I stood in the sunshine outside the gates to Disney World. I was nervous. There was no denying it. Spending the day with people I didn't know very well, if at all, was making me anxious. A little bit of apprehension melted away when I heard Jax's voice.

"Miss Richards," he yelled as he ran toward me and threw his arms around my waist. "You came," he said, looking up at me with his eyes so blue and lashes any grown woman would maim for.

"I'm here. Couldn't resist a day at Disney."

"Glad you could make it," came Devon's voice, just as deep as it'd been the day before. "Ruby," he said, turning to his daughter, standing just behind him. "You know Miss Richards."

"Hey," Ruby mumbled, obviously not too excited to see me.

"Hey, Ruby, it's nice to see you."

She didn't respond, just turned back to her father. "When is Aunt Evie supposed to be here?"

"Any minute," Devon responded. He then mouthed "Sorry," and shrugged. All I could do was smile in return.

"Aunt Evie," Jax yelled with the same enthusiasm he'd used to greet me. The same hug, in fact, as he ran to a blonde woman walking toward us.

"Jaxy," she said as she dropped to her knees to hug him back. I watched as her eyes closed and arms wound around him. She hugged him for a long time, saying things into his ear that I couldn't hear, but could see were said with love and affection. When he finally pulled away she rose, but only to wrap Ruby in a similar embrace. There was no denying that those kids loved her and she loved them right back.

"Nate," Jax said as the dark-haired man next to Evie picked him up and gave him a much rougher, more masculine hug.

"How's it going, kid? I've practiced my Minecraft skills since last time and I'm ready to kick your butt."

"Never," Jax replied with a smile.

I watched as Evie approached Devon with a shy smile and gave him a much shorter embrace, Nate shaking his hand, smiling broadly. I also noticed how Ruby seemed glued to Evie's side.

"Evie, Nate, this is Grace," Devon said, motioning toward me. He smiled, a brilliant smile that almost made me stumble, then pressed his hand lightly at the small of my back. It was the gentlest of touches, but the heat from his hand radiated throughout me. "I invited her to come along."

"Nice to meet you both." I reached out for Evie's hand first, noticing the friendly smile she gave me, which matched Nate's as he shook my hand as well.

"She's my teacher," Jax offered.

"Any friend of Devon's is a friend of ours," Evie said.

"Good to meet you," Nate said. His handshake was friendly and short, accompanied by a smile. He dropped his hand from mine and I watched as he wrapped it around Evie's waist, the move natural and smooth. I noticed she leaned into him without even thinking about it, her body molding to his without a second thought.

"Come on," Jax said excitedly. "I want to ride the merry-go-round first. Then the roller coaster around the mountain. Then Dumbo."

"Woah, buddy," Devon said, laughing. "We'll start at the beginning and work our way around, all right?"

I walked along with the group, trying hard not to feel out of place. It was strange being in such a public and busy place with a group of people I really didn't know. Well, besides Jax. I was right, however, about it being crowded. There were people everywhere and a group of six was hard to keep together. When a cluster of teenagers pushed through our little huddle, separating me from the rest, I immediately began to regret my decision to go. It must have been a group from a school because the cluster of students soon turned into a crowd. I tried to make my way through them, but I'd lost track of Devon and the rest of the group.

Suddenly, a warm hand wrapped around mine and I was being pulled forward. Devon's face finally appeared and I let out a breath I hadn't realized I was holding.

"Stay close," he said gently, his face just inches from mine.

"Okay," I said quietly. He let my hand go, of course. We couldn't walk through Disney World holding hands, but it didn't change the fact that as soon as my hand was free from his, it felt cold and empty. I wiped my palm on my thigh to try and erase the fact that he'd been there, but it didn't work. I silently followed the group, more confused than ever.

The lines were stupid long, as I'd expected, but it turned out that Devon, the kids, and Evie and Nate had a FASTPASS that got them to the front of the lines. Lots of other people had them as well, so we didn't automatically get on, but the lines were drastically shorter. I didn't have the pass, but that was all right with me, as I didn't plan on riding anything.

"You go ahead," I said to Devon as they started toward the merry-go-round. "I'll watch."

"You're not going to ride it?"

I shook my head. "I get motion sickness. I don't like rides."

He blinked at me and a confused expression crossed his face. "You don't like rides, but you came to Disney World? What for?"

I shrugged. "I like Disney. There's plenty to do aside from the rides." That was true. I did want to go to

Disney. Even if I spent the day watching Jax and Ruby have the time of their lives. But the other reason I came—the reason that scared me and wouldn't hide under the proverbial rug I kept trying to sweep it under—was simply because he'd asked. Because it meant spending a day with him. Because I feared I'd never be able to tell him no.

He looked back to where the others were moving forward in the line, then back to me.

"Go," I said with a laugh. "I don't mind. Promise. I'll watch. Take some photos even." He stared at me for just one more moment, but then Ruby called out to him, and he turned back to his children and joined them in line. I sighed and walked back to where I could watch the ride go round and round. A few minutes later the ride slowed and a new batch of riders loaded on. I smiled as Jax sped through the ride, weaving through the horses until he apparently found the perfect one. Ruby casually strolled behind him, picked a horse that seemed to do, and climbed aboard like she was doing it a favor by riding it. Devon chose the horse right beside Jax, which was a few behind Ruby. Nate and Evie picked a bench and cozily cuddled up to each other like no one else existed and the ride was built just for them. A smile pulled at my face, liking the way the two of them seemed to love each other so deeply.

The ride started and Jax bounced up and down on his horse. His eyes looked out to the crowd. I assumed he was searching for me, so when his gaze roamed in my direction I waved. His eyes locked on mine and he gave me an enthusiastic wave. I pulled out my phone and took pictures as everyone sailed past me. After two rotations my decision not to ride was reinforced as I started to feel ill, so I turned away and watched the people walking past me.

Chapter Six

Devon

Catching sight of Grace each time the ride went past her was like a shovel digging something up inside me. Why in the world would she come here just to stand by and watch us? I felt like shit for pressuring her to come now. *Damn.* I even made her buy her own ticket. I'd wanted her to say yes so badly, but I didn't think she'd come if it seemed even close to a date, so refusing to buy her ticket was more of a ploy to get her to say yes. Now I just felt like an idiot.

The ride slowed and I looked over at Jaxy again, who was all smiles. I loved seeing my kids smile. Ruby's smile, when it came around, was sweet and sincere. Someday—in the very far away future—Ruby would smile at a boy and he'd move the world to see her smile again. Jaxy's smile, however, was just pure joy and exuberance. He was all cheeks and teeth and *happiness*.

We stepped out of the gate and walked around to find Grace leaning against the fence surrounding the ride. She was looking down at her phone and I used the moment to take her in. My eyes started at the bottom and worked their way up. Her shapely legs were toned and mostly visible, as she'd worn white shorts. They weren't indecently short, but they definitely weren't made to be modest. She wore a dark blue shirt made of some material I imagined was as soft as it was billowy. It was sheer and through it I could see a white tank top with tiny straps. Her dark, shoulder-length hair was pulled back into a ponytail. She had on sunglasses, but before she'd put them on I'd noticed she wasn't wearing much makeup. Maybe just mascara. She looked fresh and clean.

The whole package was sexy as hell.

She didn't notice us until we were right in front of her. She gave me another smile and then held her phone up. On the screen was a photo of Jax and me smiling at each other, his horse up higher than mine, him looking down at me. We both looked happy. It occurred to me in that moment that since Olivia passed, there hadn't been many pictures taken of me with my kids. There was no one around to take them.

"Do you think you could text that to me?" I wanted a copy. I didn't know what I'd do with it, but I wanted it nevertheless.

"Um, sure," she said, seeming nervous for some reason, then turned the phone back around to look at the screen. I watched her thumbs moving quickly, then she handed it to me. "Just put your phone number in there."

Ah-ha. I tried not to smile as I punched in my phone number. "There you go."

She hit Send and I knew in a few moments I'd feel my phone buzz in my pocket. "Thanks."

"Dad, look!" I glanced down at Jaxy, who was pointing further into the park. "Pluto!" Sure enough, Pluto was traipsing through the park, only making it a few feet before stopping to hug children and take pictures with tourists. "Can we go meet him? Please?"

"Of course." I laughed. "That's why we're here." He grabbed my hand and practically dragged me through crowds of people until Pluto was standing right in front of us.

"Pluto!" Jaxy cried as he gave the tall dog one of his running hugs.

I smiled and then noticed Ruby standing next to me, indecision painted across her face. I gave her a nudge. "Go on." She looked up at me, rolled her eyes, and then slowly walked to join her brother, pretending to be irritated the whole time. When she approached Pluto he took his time with her, used his giant pronounced snout to sniff her out, pressing his nose into the side of her neck, making her laugh, then he pulled her into a hug. I let out a breath when she eagerly wrapped her arms around him in return.

"She's what? Eleven? You've got your work cut out for you," Grace said to me, taking in the scene with Ruby and Pluto.

"Don't I know it," I said with a chuckle. "I think she knows she got the short end of the stick, and she makes sure everyone else knows her life is hard." I let out a sigh. "I'm hoping it's a phase. If I'm lucky, by the time she gets to high school she'll realize that the hardships in life make us stronger, which means we can tackle more, not less." I looked down at Grace and was struck by her warm eyes. She'd pushed her sunglasses up to rest on top of her head, and her blue eyes were strikingly emotive.

"That's a really powerful stance to take. Is it how you really feel?" she asked, as quietly as she could and still be heard in Disney World. Her words were soft and hopeful, as if my answer were important to her.

"It has to be," I said, shrugging one shoulder. "After everything we've been through, nothing could be that hard again. It should make everything easier, right?" I watched as she considered my words, took them in, pondered them.

"I hope so," she said with a faint smile, bringing her sunglasses back down to her eyes.

It occurred to me as I watched her try to push back whatever was running through her mind, that perhaps I wasn't the only one who'd lived through something terrible.

The next few hours were spent following the children through the park. Ruby decided she didn't hate it there and actually started having a good time. She so rarely let her guard down that it was incredible to watch her laugh and smile unreservedly. My heart lurched at one point when I saw Ruby and Evie holding hands as they walked in front of us. Evelyn had always looked so similar to Olivia, especially from behind. But I was immediately drawn away from the image when Jaxy tugged me toward a food stand.

"I'm hungry, Daddy."

My watch indicated it was well past lunchtime, so I ruffled his hair and agreed it was time to eat. I called out to Ruby, Evie, and Nate, and we decided to find a table and then divide and conquer the food stands.

Nate offered to hold the table we eventually found and Jax wanted to stay with him. Ruby wanted to go with Evie, so that left Grace and me to bring back lunch for us and Jax.

"You have to let me buy you lunch. It's bad enough I made you buy your own ticket when you weren't even going to ride anything," I said, looking over at Grace, only to see her smiling.

"It's not a big deal. I'm having a good time."

"Still…," I said, unsure of how else to convince her. "Jax wants a hot dog. If you'd like something else, just speak up and we'll find another place to grab you some lunch."

"Hot dogs are great," she said, still a little too compliant.

"Are you always this agreeable?"

She shrugged and then looked down at her feet. When she looked back up at me, her cheeks were pink. "I can be disagreeable." She flattened her lips, forcing the smile from them. I assumed she was trying to look menacing, but it just didn't work. Not with the sunlight creating a halo around her dark hair and the blue of her eyes sparkling up at me.

"Sure. I'll believe it when I see it." We both chuckled and then an uncomfortable silence settled between us.

"So, Evie and Nate seem great. Jax and Ruby really seem to love them. How do you know each other?"

I should have thought about this question coming up, should have formulated some sort of answer to have ready, since it was sort of an obvious one. But I hadn't thought that far ahead. And I had no idea what to tell her. A big part of me wanted to tell her everything, but things between us were awkward enough; unloading on her in the middle of Disney World probably wasn't best. But I wanted to tell her the truth. The need to be transparent with her was overwhelming, and I didn't want to stop and think about what that meant.

"Evie was my wife's best friend." There. That was the truth. Well, part of it. The easiest part.

"Oh," she replied, with obvious surprise. "Oh," she said again, this time with a somber tone. The line moved forward and so did we.

"Yeah. She was really close with the kids before we moved here. This is only the second time they've seen her since then. She splits her time between LA and Fairbanks, where Nate lives. Well, he splits his time too. Anyway… she wanted to come see the kids."

"That's great that she still gets to see them, and that they still have that part of their mother," she said softly. For some reason, it baffled me that she'd spoken the words I'd thought almost every time Evelyn had called or Skyped with them. In the long run, the good she did for the kids far outweighed any awkwardness between us. And the awkwardness seemed to have faded and dissipated.

"I agree. I'm very grateful for Evelyn. She was one of the only reasons we made it through after Olivia passed. She did a lot for us." I hoped and prayed Grace didn't have mind reading capabilities, or that my thoughts weren't written all over my face. A lot of things had happened after my wife died, and I wasn't proud of all of them, but my past was my past.

With four hot dogs between the two of us— because I knew Jaxy would want more than one—we made our way back to the table. Evie and Ruby had beaten us back, and Ruby turned to me with a wide smile.

"Dad," she said excitedly, "Aunt Evie says she and Uncle Nate will take us over to Space Mountain next. It's supposed to be the coolest roller coaster ever. It's all in the dark."

I took my spot next to Jaxy, spreading our food out while he bit into his lunch without a second's hesitation. "Are you guys sure Space Mountain is the best ride to go on right after lunch?"

"Oh," Nate said, sucking in a breath so it hissed through his teeth. "He's got a point, babe. I know you're used to being around little kids, but I'm a sympathetic barfer and if one goes, I'm definitely going too."

"Wow," Evie said, laughing. "Just when I thought there wasn't anything else to learn about you."

"I promise I won't throw up," Jaxy swore, making everyone laugh. "No, really, last year I went to the spring break carnival with Grandma and Grandpa. I had three slices of pizza, cotton candy, *and* a milkshake, then went on the Gravitron, like, seven times. Didn't barf once."

"Jax," I said with a groan, "stop talking about throwing up. We're all trying to eat." Jaxy shrugged and then took a giant bite of his hot dog.

"I'll brave the roller coaster," Evie said with a smile. "We'll just make them sit behind us."

Chapter Seven

Grace

The last day of school was always a mixed bag of emotions. I was glad school was out, was looking forward to two months of not teaching, but that year in particular I would really miss the kids. This was the first time my life hadn't severely intruded on my work, so I'd spent one blissfully drama-free year teaching those kids, and something in my brain didn't want to let them go; didn't want the first successful year to be over.

But the summer promised to be good. Promised to be relaxing. Promised to be exactly what I imagined when I moved to Florida.

I took a job bartending in the evenings on the weekends. I wasn't looking to participate in the party that seemed to sprout up when the sun went down, but I definitely didn't have a problem making money serving alcohol to those who did. Two or three nights of tending bar gave me almost what I made in a week teaching, and I needed something to sustain me over the summer. I'd started three weekends ago, in order to be trained before summer officially started, and working both jobs was really taking a toll on me.

That, coupled with the emotional good-bye to twenty-six second graders, left me mentally and physically exhausted. Luckily, the last day of school fell on a Wednesday, so I had a day to recover before I had to go back to the night job.

I left the school building, hearing the door close with a familiar thud that felt more final than it ever had before, and the emotions started to come over me. I felt the pinching in my throat and stinging in my eyes. I didn't want to cry, but the idea of not seeing those tiny faces smiling at me every morning pulled at me. I made it to my car without a tear, but once the car door was shut behind me, one slid down each cheek. I'd wiped them away, still trying not to lose control, when I heard the ping of my phone indicating I had a text.

You're not crying outside of a school, are you?

This came from Devon and made me laugh. Since our trip to Disney I'd seen him a few times when he was picking Jax up from TAG, and we'd been texting back and forth sporadically. The texts were friendly and completely appropriate, but it didn't mean I wasn't excited to receive them. Something about attention from Devon lit me up inside, made the day-to-day seem more vibrant and exciting. From the little flutters in my stomach to the random smiles whenever he came to mind, everything about him made me happy.

Perhaps. I've heard it's cathartic.

Need some cheering up?

I stared at his message for a good minute. In all the texts we'd exchanged in the past six weeks, none of them had alluded to spending more time together. I'd thought about him a lot, but more in a lamenting way, wishing things were different. But now things *were* different, and he was basically asking me to meet up with him. I couldn't find a way to make my fingers move, or the thoughts to come up with some sort of reply. He must have figured I was having a minor panic attack because he texted me again.

Nothing fancy. Just coffee? Between friends.

Between friends? Ugh. Either I'd been friend zoned, or he was adding the emphasis to make me more comfortable. I didn't know which, but I was hoping for the latter.

Can I meet you in an hour?

The idea of meeting Devon looking like I did was terrifying. I needed to go home, shower, and regroup.

Sure. Name the place.

I sent him a link to my favorite coffee shop, Silk, and told him I'd be there in an hour.

When I entered the coffee shop, it was practically empty. I immediately spotted Devon sitting on the two-person couch in the corner. He saw me coming and stood with a smooth smile.

"Hey," he said.

"Hi," I replied as I came to a stop in front of him. There were a few seconds of awkwardness, neither one of us sure how to greet the other. Handshakes were too formal, hugs were too personal, but when he leaned down, one hand coming to rest on my elbow while his cheek pressed close to mine, I couldn't help but feel the butterflies in my stomach come awake in a flurry. A kiss on the cheek from Devon would definitely go a long way to cheer me up.

He pulled away and I couldn't help the blush that ran warm across my face.

"Can I get you something?" he asked, smile still on his face, hand still on my elbow.

"That'd be great. Vanilla latte, please. Iced."

"Got it." He gave my elbow a gentle squeeze then made his way to the counter. I took a seat on the couch, trying to look as though I was completely at ease, when I totally was not.

He returned with two cups, handing one to me, then sitting next to me on the couch, angled with one knee up so he was facing me, an arm draped along the back.

"You don't look too torn up. There must not have been many tears." He smiled just before he took a sip of his coffee.

"Only a few tears were shed. And it was expected. I'm kind of a crier. I know I'll see most of the kids again, it's just been an exceptionally great year and I'm sad to see it end."

"Look on the bright side: maybe next year's batch will be even better." He winked at me and it only made my smile spread wide across my face.

"I don't know. This year's kids were pretty spectacular."

"Jaxy is going to miss you. He told me so." Those words tugged hard on my heartstrings. "But I told him that perhaps he'd get to see you this summer sometime." Devon let the words hang in the air between us, alluding to more time spent together, and I instantly turned into a shy teenager, looking down at my coffee and smiling even wider.

Then I took in a deep breath, forced my smile to notch down from blinding to simply radiant, and shrugged one shoulder, looking back to him. "Perhaps."

We were flirting. There was no denying it. And while we'd flirted a little at Disney World, this was definitely a new level of flirtation. I wasn't opposed, and found it came back to me easily. Or perhaps it was just who I was flirting with that made it easy.

"So, have any exciting plans for the summer?" he asked, genuinely interested.

"Not really. I'm tending bar part-time on the weekends, and aside from that, I plan on reading and relaxing by the pool at my apartment."

"You took on another job?" His face twisted with confusion.

"When you sign a teaching contract, you can either take your salary split up into twelve months or ten. When I first moved here I took the ten-month deal because it was more per month and being single in Florida isn't the cheapest. So, I have to take a summer job to bridge the gap." His expression had moved from happy and flirty to concerned and even a little aggravated. "I make pretty good money bartending."

"I bet," he grumbled, and took another drink from his mug.

"Do you guys have any good summer plans?" I asked, trying to steer us from the topic that obviously upset him.

"Kids are spending the days with my mom. She's been begging to watch them more, and even though I've resisted this long, I figure two months of them might hold her over," he said, finally letting his smile come back.

"It's great that your parents are close and you can count on them for help."

"Yeah," he said, obviously thinking about his next words carefully. "Can I take you somewhere?"

His question caught me off guard. "Uh, sure," I said hesitantly.

"I just thought maybe we could go for a walk. Talk a little."

"Okay," I said softly, surprised by the sudden change in plans. He stood and held his hand out to me, helping me up. As we approached the door he stepped in front of me, pushing the door open, letting me pass by. I felt his hand gently press on the small of my back and something inside me dissolved. It had been so long since someone had taken care of me in any way. The simple act of opening a door for me sent my heart racing and I smiled because it was so *Devon*.

He led me to his SUV and again opened the door for me. I watched him walk around the front of the car and slide into the seat next to me.

"I thought we'd go to this park I take the kids to sometimes. There's a pond in the middle with a nice path that leads around it." He looked to me as if he were waiting until I agreed to start the car.

"Sounds good, although parks usually close at sundown." I looked out the window to see the sun was waning in the sky, the blue taking on a more orangey-purple hue.

"I'm willing to live on the wild side for one night if you are," he said, his smile returning and causing my stomach to flip.

"Let's go, then."

By the time we made it to the park the sun was even lower in the sky, but looking through the windshield at the sight before me, I couldn't care less.

The park was pretty massive, at least compared to what I'd envisioned in my mind. Sure, there was a playground, but there was also a picnic area, six separate basketball courts, and a soccer field. In the middle of it all was a pond with a fountain, spouting water up at least twenty feet. The path around the pond was lit with lights, as was the water shooting up from the fountain.

"This is beautiful," I said, still trying to take in all the beauty of the water and blooming flowers around it.

"Shall we?"

I pushed open my door and joined Devon in the damp, warm air of the evening, glad I'd gotten an iced drink. I followed his lead and we walked to the path, taking leisurely steps at a slow and relaxed pace.

"So, besides the second job, have any plans for the summer?" Devon asked, breaking the comfortable silence of the three minutes it took for us to make it to the path.

"Not really. I've got a lot of books I want to read, but that's about it."

He chuckled, then said, "That sounds amazing."

"I imagine you don't get a lot of free time, being a single parent."

"Tons," he said with more soft laughter. "The hour between them going to bed and me passing out is just enough time to accomplish exactly nothing." His laughter died, and then he continued. "Olivia used to be really great at planning things for the summer. Swimming lessons, soccer camps, play dates. I was pretty oblivious. I just went to work, came home, and went where she told me on weekends. It never occurred to me that keeping kids active and occupied in the summer was a full-time job."

"Sounds like she was a great mother."

I caught him nodding in my periphery. "Definitely." He was quiet for a moment—we both were. I didn't know what to say next, but he continued. "Can I tell you about her? This is strange for me—a first. I haven't met anyone I wanted to spend time with, but it feels wrong to be with you and not get it all out. Does that make sense?"

It did and it didn't; I wanted to spend time with him too, and I wanted to know about his marriage and his wife, but it didn't feel like any of my business. So I told him the truth. "I'll listen to anything you want to tell me."

He was quiet for a moment, but then he spoke and had all my attention.

"I met Olivia my junior year of college. She showed up at a party and seemed to be one of those typical freshman girls who went to frat parties to get drunk and hook up. The instant I saw her, there was something about her that pulled me to her, but she was with one of my frat brothers. I tried to brush the thoughts away, but all night I watched as she got progressively drunker and my brother got progressively handsier.

"At the end of the night I saw them going up the stairs and he was practically carrying her, she was so drunk. He looked buzzed, but definitely wasn't as gone as she was. It made me sick, so I intervened. I pretty much wrestled her away from him and she was so drunk she didn't even notice. He was pissed, called me a cock-block, and I knew my whole frat would be angry with me, but I didn't care. I took her in my room, laid her in my bed, and slept on the floor."

He paused, taking a sip of his coffee, and continued slowly on the path.

"When she woke up the next morning, she assumed we'd slept together and was treating me the way she probably treated all the guys she woke up with the next morning. She tried to brush me off, tried to act as though it wasn't a big deal, but when I explained to her what had really happened—that my fraternity brother was going to practically rape her—she just broke down on my bed. I sat with her, all day, and listened to her story. Turns out, she'd dated a guy all through high school and during her junior year he actually had raped her."

"Oh, God," I said automatically, my hand coming up to cover my mouth as I gasped. "That's terrible."

"Yeah," he agreed sullenly. "It was one of those situations where she'd said yes before, so he didn't think her screaming 'no' meant anything."

I closed my eyes and tried to push the images my mind conjured up aside. I'd never been sexually assaulted, but I could imagine the fear and anger and helplessness that came along with it.

"It went on for a couple of months before she could end the relationship, and when she left for college, all the anger she felt toward him turned into an effort to reclaim her body. She slept with guys, said yes to anyone, because saying yes was her right and she wanted to use it." He let out a large sigh and I couldn't help but feel bad for him; he was obviously upset about what she'd gone through. I wanted to comfort him in some way, but didn't know how. "Of course, that particular day we didn't work through all that. That information came in the following years. But that day, the day she woke up in my room, was the first day of us, and we were together from that day forward. I felt this need to protect her, to show her that guys could be decent, that we weren't all assholes."

It seemed fitting, the thought of Devon on a white horse, wanting to rescue a damsel in distress. His goodness was something I'd been attracted to since the very first time I met him.

"It was hard in the beginning. She tested our relationship a lot. She obviously thought, somewhere inside, I'd treat her just like all the others, that one day I'd leave her if she pushed me away hard enough, but I couldn't. I loved her because she was broken, but I also loved her because she was strong enough to take care of herself. She didn't need me, but she wanted me more than she could admit, and that made me love her even more."

I never would have thought listening to a man describe his love for someone else would make me fall for him, but I was. Hearing the way he described her, how he cared for her, how he wanted happiness for her, it went a long way to endear him to me. I wanted, so desperately, for someone to care for me that way, with that much intensity and love.

"It wasn't until Ruby was born that Olivia seemed to accept that I wasn't going anywhere, that I wanted her—flaws and all—and that she wasn't getting rid of me."

"She was lucky to have you," I said softly, saying words truer than I'd ever spoken. I didn't know Olivia, but I knew she was lucky to have Devon behind her and beside her.

He let out a loud sigh. "I know it must seem that way to you, hearing all this, but really I am the lucky one. Breaking through her boundaries was hard, but what I got in return was incredible." He smiled at me and I knew he was thinking about his children. And suddenly, before I could even try to rein it in, I was tearing up. All I could imagine was Devon and a woman who looked like an older version of Ruby, so incredibly happy, and then having it all ripped out from underneath them. How unfair it was to be given the love of a lifetime, only to have it taken away. I pictured the Devon I'd first met three years ago—the broken, sobbing, destroyed man who was in the midst of mourning.

"Devon," I whispered, a tear escaping down one cheek. "I'm so sorry."

"Hey," he said, turning to me and noticing my tears. "Come here." He wrapped his arms around me and I curled into him, keeping the hand with my coffee at his side. "No crying. I'll never get you to go out on a real date with me if I make you cry," he said, joking, rubbing his free hand up and down my back. "Don't be sad," he finally whispered right next to my ear.

"I just can't imagine," I said, pulling away and wiping under my eyes. "I'm sorry, I just remember you that night outside the school, and how upset you were."

"Yeah," he said, half groaning. "That was a dumb idea. I should never have gone that night." I nodded, agreeing. "But," he said as he dipped down, making himself eye level with me, "we might not have ever met if I didn't."

The intensity of his eyes made a ball of warmth form inside me, and I couldn't help but blush. He stood and we started walking around the pond again.

"Do you believe in fate?" he asked, his voice softer and almost wistful.

I thought about my life, of all the circumstances that had brought me to where I was in that particular moment, and the idea that it had all been predetermined was pretty depressing. I wanted it to be random, to not have to think about walking along a path that was so broken and jagged without any hope of maybe finding an alternate route.

"I don't know," I answered as honestly as I could.

"Believing that Olivia and I met for a reason, and that there's a purpose past her death, is the only thing that got me through it. I had to believe that there was more waiting for me and Ruby and Jax."

"That makes sense."

We were quiet for a few more minutes and my mind was reeling, taking in all the information he'd given me. We came upon a bench, situated to face the pond, and he motioned toward it. "Shall we?"

"Sure," I said with a slight smile, taking a seat on the bench. He sat next to me and I let out a breath.

"I'm sorry I dumped all that on you," he said, making me turn to look at him. "I learned a while ago that honesty is the best policy. There's more I want to tell you, but I don't think it needs to be said tonight."

I blinked at his candid words, wondering why the idea of a dishonest man was always the go-to, when obviously there were men in the world who viewed the truth as a necessity instead of an agenda.

"We'll have time for everything important," I whispered, still looking in his eyes.

"I hope so," he said, just as quietly. We sat on the bench for a while; the only thing heard was the splashing of the water and the rhythmic sounds of frogs croaking. The sun had set since we'd arrived, but the air was still warm and comfortable. Eventually, Devon spoke again.

"So, I've spilled all my beans for the evening. How about you?"

"Me?"

"Yeah, you," he said, smiling again. Moonlight lit his face, making him all the more handsome. "What's your story? I didn't get much information out of you at Disney World."

"Not a lot to tell," I said, hoping he believed me. There were things to tell Devon about, things I would eventually have to tell anyone I seriously considered dating, but I didn't want to drag us any further down than we already were. "I went to college for elementary education, married my college boyfriend soon after we graduated, started life together, realized life wasn't always the fairy tale you were told to expect, then moved here as soon as the divorce was final."

"Wow." He sounded surprised.

"Wow?"

"I mean…," he started, rubbing his hand along the back of his neck. "You're so young. That's a lot to go through at your age."

"You're too young to be a widower."

"That's the truth."

"I'm sorry, I'm not trying to be rude."

"No, no, you're not. I'm sorry. You just look so young and I thought…. Wait, how old are you?"

"I'm twenty-seven. Old enough to be married *and* divorced. Actually, I was married at twenty-one, divorced at twenty-four, and a Floridian shortly thereafter." The air was still between us and I heard the bouncing of a basketball from the courts at the other end of the park. I took another sip of my coffee and worked up the nerve to ask the question that was practically burning in my mouth. "Does it bother you that I've been divorced?"

I wasn't brave enough to look at him, to try and read his face before he gave his answer.

"I think what bothers me most about it is that someone was stupid enough to let you go."

I wanted to tell him everything in that moment, but the overwhelming urge to not ruin all I felt between us won out. *There will be plenty of time to ruin it.*

"Hey," he said softly as his hand wrapped gently around the back of my neck, and my eyes slowly fluttered up to meet his gaze. "I'm not doing a great job of cheering you up, am I?"

I let out a small laugh. "Death and divorce are my top two favorite topics of conversation." He laughed with me and I almost lost my breath as his thumb moved up and down the sensitive skin of my neck. His hold on me was gentle, yet firm, and I wasn't complaining. It had been a long time since a man's fingers had trailed over any part of me, and I both loved and hated how wonderful it felt.

"Shall we finish our lap around the pond?" His voice was soft and I got the impression that walking around the pond wasn't actually what he wanted to do. I hadn't been with many men, but I could tell when one wanted to kiss me. Devon's eyes were dark, hooded, and darting down to my lips with every other loud thump of my heart. And even though kissing Devon seemed like a great distraction from all the bad, I knew if we were going to have a first kiss, I didn't want it to be in the wake of the death and divorce speeches.

We made it back to Devon's car, the rest of the walk uneventful but enjoyable; Devon made sure to keep the conversation light, telling me funny stories about Jax and Ruby. I had a few gems to tell him myself, what with my entire workweek full of eight-year-olds.

Just before he opened the door for me, he asked, "Can I take you out on a real date? Wednesday night, maybe? Dinner? A movie?"

"Sure," I said, trying not to blush. "I'd like that."

Chapter Eight

Devon

I hastily pulled into a parking spot outside Grace's apartment building and cringed when the car slammed into the sidewalk. I pushed open the door as I turned the car off, and walked as quickly as I could without looking like someone was chasing me. I found the door with her apartment number on it and knocked.

Grace opened the door with a beautiful smile and before she could do or say anything, I started apologizing.

"I'm so sorry, Grace. The kids took forever to get ready. Jax couldn't find his left shoe, and Ruby was not only moving the slowest I've ever seen her move, but she also had the worst attitude. I'm sorry."

"Really, it's fine," she said, still smiling as she stepped out into her breezeway.

"It's not fine," I said to her back as she turned to lock her dead bolt.

"Devon, it's thirty minutes. You texted me and let me know you'd be late. It's not like I don't understand how children are the ultimate time suckers." Her laugh rang out, echoing around us, making my nerves, which had previously been completely raw, calm. I was immediately at ease.

I was also immediately noticing the dress Grace was wearing.

There was nothing overtly sexual about the dress, but everything about Grace was sexy. The way the soft blue fabric crossed over her front, cutting right between her breasts. Or the way it hugged her waist and hung perfectly from her ass.

I couldn't remember the last time I purposely looked at a woman's ass.

The bottom of the dress flared out slightly when she turned, letting me take in the length of her legs.

"You look amazing," I stammered before I could stop myself.

"Thanks," she replied shyly. "You look pretty great too."

I looked down at my white cotton button-up shirt and jeans. Nothing special about me. Guys had it easy in the What to Wear on a Date department.

I led the way to my SUV, opening the door for her, watching as she nimbly folded herself in, giving me another shy smile. I crossed in front and climbed in, turning to her with another apology on the tip of my tongue.

"We can't make the early movie, but we can get dinner and hope we make the later showing. I'm sorry, again."

"Dinner sounds great, Devon. And it's fine. No more sorrys."

We talked all the way to the restaurant and the conversation flowed effortlessly, which only made me more nervous. I wanted the evening to go well, for us to be comfortable around each other and for everything to go smoothly. It was scary how much I wanted all that. It had taken me long enough to come to terms with the fact that I wanted to take Grace out on a date, and now that the official date was happening, I was prepared for disaster—for some cosmic joke to play out and to hear the laughter ring inside my head, saying, "You didn't think dating would be *easy*, did you?"

But aside from the late arrival, so far it was smooth sailing.

I didn't know what to do with goodness—it had evaded me for so long.

Still, there we were, driving to dinner, talking, and nothing terrible was happening. Grace laughed as she told me stories about all the drunken college kids she'd served over the weekend, and I entertained with my account of the elderly woman who'd come into my hardware store looking for a chain saw to take down the tree in her front yard that blocked her view of the hunky swimsuit models that lived across the street.

"She did not!" Grace teased, laughing as I pulled into a parking spot at the one good Italian restaurant in town. That time I managed not to ram my car into any cement dividers.

"She did. And even though it went against my better judgment, I couldn't find a valid reason to not sell her a chain saw."

I listened to her laughter as I climbed out of the car and then opened her door for her. I held out my hand to help her out, and when she placed her hand in mine it was as if every part of me was aware of it: my heart rate increased, the hairs on the back of my neck stood up, and my mouth ran dry. My whole being was completely attuned to the fact that her hand was in mine and it felt incredible. Once she was on her own two feet, I let her hand fall away, even though it almost hurt to lose the contact.

We walked into the restaurant and, luckily, were led to an open table. The waiter took our drink order and then we were left to each other once again.

"So," I said, trying to keep the conversation going. "What made you want to be a teacher?" A smile started in the corner of her mouth, a small one, and I could tell she was trying to hide it, but she couldn't contain it and eventually it shone brightly. "What's so funny?"

"Do you know how many times I've been asked that question? Something about teachers, I guess. Everyone always asks that. I imagine investment bankers don't get the same question. Or mechanics."

"Maybe it has something to do with the entire universe understanding that teachers get royally screwed when it comes to pay and appreciation. I think people are interested in why someone would willingly sign up for a job that doesn't get the thanks it deserves."

"Perhaps," she said in a way that made me think she didn't agree. "Or maybe it's that everyone thinks I'd have to be crazy to willingly become a second-grade teacher," she said with a laugh.

"Is that it? Are you crazy?"

"No," she said on a sigh, her gaze slowly falling to her hands, clasped together and resting on the table. "I just really love children." Her words were somber and sad; a blaring contradiction to the laughter just seconds before, and even the words themselves.

"Well, I'd say you picked a great job, then."

"Yeah." A hint of a smile returned.

I thought about my career choices and how none of them were born out of love—well, not really. I went into business consultation for the money. I had a kid on the way and I had a mind for it, so consulting seemed like a good place to start. And it was. That job allowed our family to have a good start—a nice home, a stay-at-home mom for my kids, vacations, and nice cars. But a few months after Olivia died I realized I couldn't be that same guy anymore. I wasn't the go-to-work dad, who could come home to a meal on the table and freshly bathed children I could tickle and play with for an hour before bedtime. I was now mother and father. And even though I came into my new role in the worst way possible, I wouldn't give it up. I would gladly take a job I didn't even need a degree for if it meant I could watch my kids grow up, be there every step of the way, and see every gruesome and wonderful moment.

So even though I didn't necessarily take the job at my dad's store out of love for the career, I took it out of love for my kids and needing to make that change for all of us.

We ordered our meals and I tried to steer clear of topics that would take the smile off her face again.

Grace was on her second glass of wine and the new rosy color of her cheeks only made her more attractive. The food had come and gone, dessert had been shared, and even though we could have made it to the movie, neither one of us moved to leave. I was enjoying her too much to risk ruining it by sitting in a dark room where I couldn't even look at her. From my seat across a small table, I could watch her smile, listen to her laugh, and study the way her expressive eyebrows gave more away about her than her words did sometimes. I could watch the way she absentmindedly moved her hand through hair that looked incredibly soft, only to watch it fall right back into place, framing her face.

My phone buzzed in my pocket and when I pulled it out I noticed the time and my mother's number. I figured the kids wanted to say good night before my mom put them to bed.

"I should take this," I said with apology in my voice. She just smiled in reply and took another sip of her wine. "Hey, Mom," I said, speaking through my own smile.

"Devon, I'm really sorry to call and interrupt, but Ruby's pretty sick and I need to know what you want me to do about it."

"What do you mean she's sick?" The smile disappeared from my face, quickly replaced with a furrowed brow and concern burning in my chest.

"She's been sick since about twenty minutes after you dropped them off. She said her stomach ached, then she just started throwing up. She's vomiting every ten to fifteen minutes. Her body is trying to work something out of her system, but vomiting at this rate for three hours? She'll be severely dehydrated if we can't get some fluids in her, and every time I make her take a sip of water, she just gets sick again. I think she needs to go to the ER to get an IV."

"Shit," I whispered, partly upset my mom had to deal with my sick child, but mostly upset I wasn't there with Ruby when she was so sick. I'd come to learn that 90 percent of parenting was dealing with guilt.

"Can we get a check?" I heard Grace ask our waiter, and I was grateful she understood our date was effectively over.

I used one hand to throw some bills on the table, then shove my wallet back in my pocket and stand up.

"I'll be there soon. Just hang tight and I'll come get her."

"Devon, I can handle a sick child. You don't have to cut your date short."

I appreciated what my mom was doing, but I couldn't stay out with Grace knowing Ruby was so sick.

"I know you can, Mom, but I'm her dad. This is my job. Your job is to feed them sugar and send them home crazy. Don't worry about my date. There will be

more. I'll be there soon. Tell Ruby to hang in there."
We said our good-byes and then I hung up, shoving my
phone in my pocket as well.

"Ruby's sick?" Grace's voice was soft and full
of worry.

"Yeah," I said with a sigh, watching as she
stood and draped the strap of her purse over one bare
shoulder. Was it a bad time to notice the sexy dusting
of freckles there? Like she'd spent a lot of summers in
the sun as she grew up. "This is how Ruby's body
operates. She hardly ever gets sick, but when she does,
her whole body shuts down and she goes from fine to
really sick in just a few hours."

"Oh no," she whispered as we walked out of the
restaurant and toward my car.

"I'm really sorry," I said as I backed out of my
spot. "I was having a really great time. I'll drop you off
really quick."

"You don't have to drop me off," she responded
with quick words. "If Ruby is as sick as you say, you
need to go get her."

"I'll probably just be going straight to the ER.
Trust me, with a vomiting child—the fewer stops the
better."

"Devon, go get her. Getting her to the doctor is
most important. We'll figure everything else out later."

I stared at her. The rosiness was gone from her
cheeks, worry now present in her eyes, and I couldn't
believe she was begging to help take my child to the
emergency room.

"Okay," I said on a breath, then turned the car
toward my parents' house.

I opened the door to my parents' house and was greeted by the familiar sound of Ruby groaning in agony. Then came unmistakable sound of retching. I raced into the living room, trying to prepare myself for what was coming. Sick kids were the worst. Not only were they helpless, but they made you feel helpless too. As a rational adult, I knew sickness passed and eventually I'd start to feel better. Kids lacked that little nugget of common sense and all sicknesses were akin to dying slowly.

"Daddy," Ruby moaned as my mom wiped her mouth with a washcloth. "I don't feel well."

"I see that, baby." I knelt in front of her and put my hand to her forehead.

"She doesn't have a fever," my mom supplied kindly, her voice full of worry and concern. "She just said her stomach hurt, wouldn't eat dinner, and then…."

"Okay," I said, offering my mother a poor excuse for a smile.

"Miss Richards," Jax yelled, shooting off my father's recliner and wrapping his arms around Grace's thighs in an enthusiastic hug.

"Hey, Jax. It's good to see you."

"Are you coming to the hospital with us?"

"That's the plan," Grace said with an exhale.

"Hello, there," my mom said, in a tone that let me know immediately that she knew Grace was my date and I was interested in her.

"Mom," I said coolly, "this is Grace. Grace, my mother, Carolyn."

"It's nice to see you again," Grace said, reaching her hand out to my mom, leaving her other hand on Jaxy's back since he was still hugging her. I gave her a puzzled look and she explained. "We met at parent-teacher conferences a while ago."

"Oh, right," I said, my brain to occupied by Ruby to put all the pieces together."

"You can leave Jaxy here, Devon. There's no reason to take him to the emergency room." My mother's words broke through my mental fog.

"I want to go with Miss Richards," Jaxy whined.

"Why is Jaxy's teacher here?" Ruby asked, sounding absolutely miserable.

"She just came to help. She's going to sit with Jaxy while we take you to see the doctor." I could tell Ruby didn't buy my story. She was eleven, not five. But before she could ask me anything else, another round of sickness overcame her.

Chapter Nine

Grace

Jax and I had managed to play at least thirty games of tic-tac-toe, made countless paper airplanes, and eventually I convinced him to stretch out on the little couch with a blanket I had asked a nurse to get for him. He begged me to sit with him, and as I'd learned being his teacher, when Jaxy was sweet and wanted something, it was hard to deny him.

His head was on my lap, his blond hair starkly contrasting against the blue of my dress, and his little body was cocooned by the itchy cotton blanket anyone could identify as belonging in a hospital. I'd managed to keep him away from all the other patients, sequestering us at the far end of the waiting room, trying to keep him as germ free as one could be in the emergency room.

Devon had been back in a room with Ruby for hours and I'd heard not one peep. I hadn't expected any updates, really, but I was left wondering if everything was going all right and if Ruby was sicker than perhaps Devon had originally thought. As the minutes ticked by I became more and more concerned.

I busied myself by threading my fingers through Jax's hair. Hair that was impossibly soft. His mouth was open just slightly and tiny snores were coming from him. It was the sweetest thing I'd ever witnessed.

I heard the motorized sound of the doors opening, and when I looked up I saw Devon walking toward us, Ruby by his side. She was no longer in the clothes she'd worn in, but instead was wearing what looked like two hospital gowns: one on the right way—opening in the back—and the other on backward so it looked more like a robe.

Seeing the two of them walking side by side only made Devon's height more apparent. I knew he was tall—over six feet, easily—but next to Ruby he looked even more massive. Somewhat like a gentle giant, his hand resting on Ruby's shoulder, looking like it was there for equal parts comfort for Ruby and protection by Devon. He was taking care of her.

"They've finally released us," he said as he came to a halt in front of us. I watched as his eyes swept over Jax's sleeping form and suddenly I felt self-conscious that I'd let him fall asleep on my lap.

"He was tired." I winced inwardly at the stupidity of my words—of course he was tired.

"Thank you for helping out tonight." The sincerity in his voice caused my gaze to meet his and my heart lurched a little. Devon looked exhausted, but he also looked grateful.

"My pleasure." I moved to wake up Jax, but Devon stopped me.

"I've got it," he said, just before he slid his arm between Jax's head and my leg. The brush of his skin against me did stupid things to my heart rate, especially when I silently told myself he was just picking up his son. Effortlessly, I might add. Just swooped right down there and picked up his eight-year-old like he weighed nothing. I gently pulled the blanket off Jax and followed Devon and Ruby toward the exit. I placed the loosely folded blanket on the admin desk and gave the nurse there a smile as we passed.

"How are you feeling, Ruby?" I asked as we approached the car.

"Tired," she responded, not unkindly, but definitely as if she was exhausted and couldn't put together more than that one-word answer. I couldn't blame her. I was tired too.

We all loaded into the car, Devon buckling Jax into his booster seat while Jax mumbled in his sleepy state. Once Devon was in his seat he looked over at me, giving me a defeated smile. Before I could stop myself I reached over and gave his leg a squeeze, trying to tell him with one action that everything was all right. That just because the date didn't go as planned, it didn't mean I was pulling away.

"I just want to go to sleep," Ruby said, interrupting the moment that passed between Devon and me. I swiped my hand off his leg and watched as he turned around, his large frame filling so much of the car.

"I know, baby," he said softly. "But I've got to take Grace home and we have to stop at the drug store real quick to get you some Gatorade and your medicine."

"But I'm tired," Ruby whined, the utter desperation in her voice breaking my heart.

"Devon, this is silly. Go home. I can get a cab."

"You're not taking a cab, Grace."

"It's not a big deal. Ruby needs to go to bed." He looked like he didn't know how to make the right decision, as if he were torn between two bad choices.

"Ruby will be fine for another thirty minutes," he said, pulling out of the parking lot.

I looked back at her and I knew that even if she *would* be fine, she wasn't fine at that moment. She looked sick and exhausted, and all I wanted, more than anything, was to take her home and let her go to bed.

"How about we all go back to your place, then I'll take your car and run your errands. I don't mind," I pleaded. Something inside me needed to help, to do something to make Ruby's pain go away. A part of me ached to nurture her any way I could.

"You're not going to run my errands," he said, just as stubborn as before.

"Okay, then let me stay with the kids while you run the errands. She needs to go home." I watched as his eyes moved to the rearview mirror, assessing Ruby, then Jax.

"If we take them home, then we're there all night," he said quietly, so that only I could hear him. "I won't be able to take you home until the morning."

"I don't mind," I said insistently, trying to communicate, again, that I wanted to help.

He searched my eyes for just a moment, then finally responded with a resigned, "All right."

By the time we pulled up to his house, both kids were fast asleep. But as soon as the engine turned off, Jax's eyes opened and he sat up straight.

"Are we home?" he asked, his voice rough and sleepy.

"Yeah, bud. Can you walk yourself into the house?" Devon asked. Jax nodded in response and pushed open his door. Ruby, on the other hand, was out cold.

I watched as Devon managed to pick Ruby up and carry her in the house. I followed them in and took a seat on the couch, observing as he quietly and efficiently put Ruby to bed and then helped Jax brush his teeth and go to bed as well. When he emerged from Jax's room, shutting the door slowly to minimize the sound of it latching into place, he made his way toward me in the living room.

I sat on the couch just staring at him, waiting for whatever he had planned next. There was a coffee table between us, but I could see most of him. His hands were braced on his hips, his head hung low, shoulders slumped. He looked just as exhausted as the children had. But then his head came up and he caught my gaze.

"You sure you're all right hanging out here for a few while I run to the store?"

I tried really hard to hold in my sigh of relief that he was going to allow me to help him. "Yes. Totally and completely all right."

He pulled his car keys out of his pocket, then ran his other hand through his hair. "When I get back I'll get you set up in my room and I'll sleep on the couch."

I nodded, knowing full well I wasn't going to kick him out of his bed, but I wasn't about to argue with him about it in that moment.

"Feel free to watch TV. The remotes are right here on the coffee table. The bathroom is just down the hall, there's stuff in the fridge if you get hungry or thirsty—"

"Devon, I'll be fine. The kids will be fine. I promise."

"Yeah, okay," he said as he rubbed the back of his neck. "I'll be back as soon as I can." I watched him walk to the door, giving me a short wave before he shut it behind him, then I sat in his dark living room. It only took a few minutes before I started yawning, so I stood up and tried to walk around to keep myself awake. I walked down the hallway, peeking into the kids' rooms, checking to make sure they were still sleeping peacefully.

After I'd done a few laps around the darkened house, I finally decided to lie on the couch and read a book on my phone.

When I woke, it took me a moment to remember I was in Devon's house, but it became clear very quickly. I didn't even have to move my head to see the giant portrait of his wife hanging on the wall.

She was beautiful. She looked a lot like Ruby. I could even see a little Jax in her. But, God, she was stunning. Laughing in the shot, presumably unaware of the camera, with strands of pearls dripping through her fingers.

I tore my eyes from her, trying to push down the irrational jealousy. I would not be jealous of a woman who lost her life to cancer. What kind of person would that make me? I pushed the blanket off me, then realized I hadn't fallen asleep with a blanket. Warmth flooded me thinking about Devon draping a blanket over me in the middle of the night.

Sitting up, I took in the rest of the house that I hadn't really paid attention to the night before.

The house was nice and it looked homey. The furniture looked worn, as if people lounged on it often. The coffee table wasn't perfectly lined up with the couch, which wasn't perfectly lined up with the accent rug underneath, which only made me think that things were thrown off kilter as children ran by. I pictured Ruby chasing Jax, his side catching on the couch as he ran from her, knocking it a few inches, and nobody coming by to fix it. There were a few toys scattered around, a few books that looked to be Ruby's, and just general life litter: mail, shoes, jackets. There was no coatrack, so the coats were hanging over the chairs.

It wasn't messy—it was lived in.

Standing, I noticed the mantel had many more pictures of Olivia, only these were photos of her with her family, and I couldn't help the smile that came over my face, the deep and hollow feeling that settled in my gut, or the frown that came with feeling two warring emotions at once.

I found the bathroom and on my way back out I practically ran into Ruby.

"Oh my goodness," I said, hand to my chest, breaths coming hard and fast. "You scared me."

"I didn't know you were here." Ruby's tone landed somewhere between apologetic and accusatory.

"I fell asleep while your dad was getting your meds." For some reason, it felt as though I was trying to explain to my father why I'd missed curfew.

Ruby watched me for a few more moments, still at the threshold of the bathroom. "I'm hungry," she finally said, her voice softer, and my shoulders sagged as the tension between us melted away.

"Well, I think it would be good to let your daddy sleep for a bit, so how about I make you breakfast?"

She shrugged. "Okay." I let out a breath of relief and made my way to the kitchen, quietly opening cabinets to try and figure out what I could make for a child recovering from a stomach bug. When I heard footsteps coming down the hall, I turned just in time to see Ruby hike herself up onto one of the barstools. Then she just stared at me.

"What do you feel like eating?" She shrugged again. "Hmmm, I know when kids are sick, you're only supposed to feed them food on the BRAT list."

"The what?" Her face contorted in confusion.

"BRAT—bananas, rice, applesauce, and toast. Rice isn't a very good breakfast choice. How about toast?" I gave her a hopeful look.

"I hate toast."

"Okay...." I turned back to the cupboards, looking for applesauce but coming up empty-handed. My gaze moved over the countertops until I found what I was looking for. "Ah! But there are bananas. How about a banana?"

Ruby chewed on her bottom lip a bit, then said, "I'm, like, *really* hungry."

"Hmmm," I said, thinking that breakfast couldn't always be this difficult. Then my eyes caught something else in the cupboard. "How about banana pancakes?"

Her eyebrows rose. "You can make banana pancakes?"

I shrugged one shoulder. "Sure. It can't be that hard. You've got bananas and pancake mix. Besides, everything is possible with Google." She gave a little laugh and I wanted to hold on to that sound forever, just grab it tightly and listen to it over and over again. Instead, I walked to the coffee table to retrieve my phone.

Twenty minutes later I had thrown together Google's easiest banana pancake recipe and two good-sized pancakes were cooking on the stovetop.

"Were you on a date with my dad last night?" Ruby had been noticeably quiet as I prepared the batter, and I'd let the silence between us linger, unsure of where to start a conversation, so I was completely caught off guard by her question.

"We... were... just spending some time together. No big deal." I tried to sound airy and light, not at all like we were talking about the huge change Ruby had picked up on.

"He put on his fancy cologne before he left. And you're wearing a dress."

I read between the lines of what she was saying, and thanked my lucky stars I was forced to watch the pancakes bubble instead of having to face her. Obviously, Devon hadn't explained to his children that he was dating, and it wasn't my business to have that conversation with his daughter. The pancakes made a satisfying sizzle as I flipped them, and then I turned to Ruby.

"Your father and I just enjoy each other's company. Sometimes it's good for adults to spend time with other adults."

Her face didn't change with my statement, and she continued to watch me, looking as though she was waiting for more of an explanation. Waiting for me to tell her something that would take the fear of change away.

"Are you making us breakfast? Why are you making breakfast? What are you doing here?" Jax's questions came just as quickly as his presence. Suddenly, he was just there, climbing on the stool beside Ruby.

"Good morning, Jax. I hope you like banana pancakes."

"We've never had banana pancakes before," he replied, thankfully dropping his previous line of questioning. "But I like bananas, and pancakes, so sounds good."

I smiled at him, glad things were so black and white for him.

"Where do you guys keep your plates?"

The next few minutes were spent making sure the pancakes didn't burn, getting plates ready, finding the syrup, and then watching Ruby and Jax take their first bites.

"So?" I asked, curious as to whether the banana pancakes would pass the kid test. Both Ruby and Jax's eyes rolled closed.

"These are the best pancakes I've ever had, Miss Richards," Jax said, mouth full and with a second bite on its way.

"I'm glad you like it. And tell you what—if we're not at school, you can just call me Grace."

He nodded and gave a grunt in response.

"Ruby? How are the pancakes?" She took a moment to think about her answer.

"They'd be better with chocolate chips," she said just before putting another forkful in her mouth.

"Yeah! Chocolate chips would be amazing," Jax agreed.

I gave them both a smile. "Next time I'll be sure to add chocolate chips."

Chapter Ten

Devon

The sound of talking and laughter coming down the hall was what woke me. My eyelids were heavy, and my body was begging me to just roll over and go back to sleep, but in the last three years, that had never been an option. If the kids were up, I was up.

I remembered coming home the night before after my hasty trip to the drug store in town, walking into a dark house, the only light the moon shining in through the windows in the living room. Grace was curled up on her side, shoes slipped off her feet, cell phone on the floor just below her outstretched hand, indicating she'd fallen asleep while looking at it.

Her hair was spread out on the decorative pillow, her dress covering everything important but giving me a nice look at her legs. She looked peaceful and comfortable, prompting an inner battle; I wanted to move her to my bed and take the couch myself, but I didn't want to disturb her since she was already asleep. I'd picked up her cell phone and placed it on the coffee table, and then grabbed an extra blanket from the closet and draped it over her carefully, trying not to wake her.

After watching her sleep for a few moments, I finally dragged myself back to my room. In any other situation I would have had a hard time sleeping while Grace was just down the hall, but I'd been exhausted and I hardly remembered actually crawling into bed.

My eyes swung to the digital alarm clock I kept on my bedside table and I had to look twice. It was 10:00 a.m. The last time I'd slept until ten in the morning had been back in college. I flung the covers off the bed, pulled on a T-shirt and jeans from a pile in the corner, made my way to the bathroom, and then out to the living room.

The surprises kept coming as I walked into a scene of Grace sitting on my couch with both my kids, all of them looking at our television, watching Jax play Minecraft.

"Good morning," I said, still confused, when Grace and Ruby turned to look at me, both of them wearing perfect smiles.

"Grace made banana pancakes if you want some, Daddy. We saved you some. We just have to warm them up."

"Banana pancakes?" I asked, looking to Grace, who was still smiling.

"They are so good, Daddy. I'll go warm them up for you," Ruby said, jumping up from the couch and walking past me into the kitchen.

"You're feeling better, then?"

"Much better," she said with her head in the refrigerator.

"There's Gatorade in there. I want you to drink some of that anyway."

"I already had a whole bottle. Grace made me drink it with breakfast."

"I tried to stick to the BRAT diet, but we figured banana pancakes were a good compromise. Although, Jax has requested next time we add chocolate chips."

I was frozen where I stood, trying to take everything in.

"You made my kids breakfast?"

"Well, I was already awake, and Ruby was hungry. I figured she needed something in her belly, considering...."

I heard her trying to defend herself and I could have kicked myself for making her feel like she'd done something wrong.

"Thank you," I managed, interrupting her unnecessary apology. "It's been a while since I was able to sleep in." She smiled, but I still felt like shit. "Kids, we've got to drive Grace home, so why don't you get dressed."

"You've got to eat your pancakes," Ruby insisted, the microwave dinging.

"I'll eat them while you get changed." Ruby placed the pancakes in front of me on the bar and as she passed I stopped her, bringing her head to my chest, looking down at her. "You feeling okay, kiddo?" She didn't feel warm and the color was back in her face.

"I feel much better, Daddy. I was really hungry when I woke up, so Grace made me pancakes and made me drink the Gatorade. I feel fine."

I leaned down and pressed a kiss to her forehead. "I'm glad. Now go get dressed." She made her way down the hall and when I knew both kids were in their rooms, I turned back to Grace.

"Listen," I said, dragging my fingers through my hair, "I'm really sorry about all this. Last night was a disaster and then this morning...." I looked up at her to see the smile still fixed on her face. "This definitely wasn't the way I wanted our date to go."

She shrugged. "It's not a big deal, Devon. I hope I didn't overstep any boundaries though."

"No. No, of course not. I just don't want you to think I brought you here to take care of my kids. I didn't. I'm grateful you did, but you've got to know I didn't even think about it. It's been years since those kids didn't come right into my bedroom when they woke up. I never expected they'd come to you first."

"All right," she said, standing from the couch and walking toward me. "We're both sorry and it all worked out."

Her dress flowed around her knees and some of her hair had come loose from the bun she'd wrapped it up in. Strands fell in soft sweeps along her neck and I wanted so badly to just run a finger along her there. With both excitement and apprehension, I'd envisioned a very different ending to our evening the night before. I would have walked her to her door, found some reason to hold her hand or rest my hand on her waist, and pulled her in to me for a hug. I'd imagined kissing her, but wasn't sure if we were there yet. The last thing I wanted was to kiss Grace and then realize I wasn't ready to kiss someone who wasn't Olivia. I wanted to be *sure*.

What I hadn't anticipated was the way I would feel about Grace stepping in and taking care of my kids. It felt right. Easy. Comfortable.

And the pancakes were out of this world.

"Grace," I said between bites, "these taste incredible."

She sat on the stool right next to me and rested her chin on her hand. "I just googled an easy recipe." She gave another shrug, as if to say it was no big deal.

"You've never made these before?"

"Nope. I just saw your bananas and figured they'd be easy on Ruby's tummy."

Something deep in my chest tightened with her words. Before I could change my mind I leaned forward and kissed her, my lips pressing softly just to the corner of her mouth. She tensed at first. I hoped she was just surprised by my random advance. When I felt her relax against me, I kissed her fully. My mouth lined up perfectly with hers.

It was a soft and quick kiss, but it rocked me. After a few moments, when we both pulled away, she was still smiling when she said, "You taste like bananas and syrup."

We watched as Grace made her way up to her door, giving us a wave before she disappeared into it.

I'd wanted to walk her to her door, wanted to make at least one thing about our date normal, but with Ruby and Jax in tow it wasn't ideal. So we'd settled for a good-bye in the car, both of us staying in our own seats, but her smile and her eyes told me she was feeling the same as me; wishing I could walk her and we could get another tiny moment alone.

I pulled out of the parking lot, trying to think if there was anything that absolutely had to be done that day. Not thinking of anything pressing, I said to the kids, "You guys wanna have a lazy pajama day at home? Pizza for dinner?"

"Yay," Jaxy yelled, obviously enthused with the idea.

"I'm always down for a lazy day if pizza is involved," Ruby agreed.

I exhaled, relief puffing out with my breath. I hadn't realized how tense I'd been. But hearing the kids answer with their usual easiness made something inside me relax. It had been a crazy fifteen hours, and I was glad the kids were game to relax.

"You still feeling all right, Ruby?"

"Yeah," she answered quickly, giving me a small smile in the rearview mirror. That was typical Ruby. She didn't get sick often, but when she did it was like a tidal wave. It rolled in quick, tore her apart, and then rolled out just as quickly. There had been many nights Olivia had stayed up with her, doting on her, refusing to sleep because she knew the next round of sickness was only minutes away. I'd offered to stay up with her, but she would always wave me away, insisting that only one of us needed to be sleep-deprived, that she would need me to be rested to take care of Jaxy in the morning. Olivia's biggest transformation came with motherhood.

It didn't surprise me later when I came upon Ruby sleeping on the couch. She might have felt all right, but her body was still feeling the effects of her illness. Jax was outside, jumping on the trampoline I'd purchased the first spring we'd lived in this house. After their mother died, I found myself trying and doing anything to ease big transitions. New school? Brand-new bikes. New house? Big trampoline. I knew I couldn't buy them things to ease every one of their pains, but sometimes it made *me* feel better too. Like, at least I could give them *something*, even if I could never give them their mother back.

"Dad." I heard Ruby's voice right after I'd turned to head back to my bedroom. I turned around again and saw her still lying on the couch, but now her eyes were open and she was looking at me.

"Yeah, baby?"

"Were you on a date with Grace?"

My stomach bottomed out at her question. I had thought, after the uneventful morning, the kids hadn't thought much about Grace's presence, but apparently I was wrong. The only thing I was completely sure of in that moment, was that I had no idea how to handle it.

I walked back to the couch and lifted Ruby's feet enough to slide under them, letting her legs rest over my lap.

"Sometimes adults just like to spend time with other adults," I said slowly, just trying words on to see if they fit, if Ruby would accept them.

"That's what Grace said, too."

My head tilted and my eyebrows drew together. "You spoke to Grace about it?"

"I asked her if you guys were on a date. She said the same thing, that grown-ups just like to spend time with other grown-ups."

She asked Grace, too? I ran my hand over my face, trying to buy a little time.

"I like Grace" were my next brilliant words. "I think she's nice. What do you think?"

Ruby shrugged. "She's nice enough." Her voice was low and I knew she wasn't being completely honest with me about her feelings.

"But...?"

"It just surprised me that she was still here, I guess."

"Listen, last night I *was* out with Grace, but then you got sick and all my plans got rearranged really fast. I never intended to have Grace spend the night, but she wanted to help and it was either let her stay here, or take you kids to drive her home."

Ruby blinked at me, eyes wide and understanding.

"In all honesty," I said, then released a huge breath, trying to brace myself for a hard conversation. "Grace and I *were* on a date."

Ruby didn't say anything at first, but I couldn't help but notice that at my words her chest stopped moving. She was still for a very long moment, and then her breath came whooshing out. Her eyes filled with tears.

Shit.

"Ruby, honey, don't cry."

"Do you love her?" she whispered, the words surrounded by cries.

"Love her? Ruby, no. It was just one date." I lifted her legs and scooted closer until she was forced to sit up, now fully in my lap, her head resting against my chest. "What's wrong?"

"My friend Zoey from school said that when her dad married her stepmom, she just, like, all of a sudden was at their house all the time. Like one day she was there and the next day they were married."

I rolled my eyes while still running my hand down her back, trying to soothe her. "Zoey is a liar, Ruby. We've talked about this before. She was very likely exaggerating. I'm not in love with Grace, we're not getting married tomorrow, and you're not getting a stepmom."

"Not tomorrow, anyway," she said, pointedly.

I didn't really know how to respond. I couldn't promise her she'd never have a stepmother.

"You don't have to worry about that. I promise."

"Why not?" she asked, sniffling as she ran her hand across her nose the way kids did that made adults cringe.

"Because if I ever decide to get married again, it won't be a surprise. I won't spring someone on you and force you to love her. You won't have to fit with her because she'll fit into this family like a puzzle piece. But, honestly, Grace and I are just spending time together because we like one another, not because we're thinking about getting married."

Ruby was quiet for a few moments and all I could hear were the rhythmic sounds of Jaxy jumping on the trampoline.

"If you marry someone, will I have to call her mommy?" Ruby's voice cracked on the last word and it was almost as if someone reached into my chest and put a death grip on my heart.

"Sweetheart," I said, rocking her back and forth, holding her as close as I could. "No one will ever replace your mother. No one. Nobody will ever make you forget your mother, and nobody will ever make me forget my wife."

"Then why do you have to go on a date with someone?"

"Because, well, it's hard to explain."

"Try."

I had to hold in a small laugh because in that moment she sounded exactly like her mother—bossy.

"People, adults, they're not meant to spend their lives alone."

"You're not alone," she immediately pointed out. "You've got me and Jaxy. And Grandma and Grandpa."

"No, you're right, I'm not alone. And being with you and Jaxy doesn't make me feel alone. I love my life with you guys. But, that doesn't mean I don't miss being with someone like your mother."

"You mean like kissing and stuff." Her words were not a question; she knew exactly what she meant.

I pushed gently on her shoulders until she moved away from me so I could look her in the eyes. I moved my face down and looked at her straight on. "You're eleven years old, Ruby, so I'm not going to treat you like a baby right now. So, yes, kissing and stuff. But it's not just about that. Adults need to be around other adults for lots of reasons." What I couldn't tell her was that sometimes, after a particularly long day, I missed being able to just *talk* to someone. To have someone around who asked me about my day. Or wasn't under the age of twelve. And perhaps until I met Grace for the second time, I hadn't even realized how much I needed it.

"Are you going to go out with her again?"

Honesty had to be my best policy and I needed to be up-front with Ruby. Jax was a different story. I would have to play him by ear when it came to Grace, but I knew I had to lay it out for my daughter.

"I don't know for sure. I know I want to see her again, but it all depends on whether we've scared her away already."

Ruby laughed at my joke, and I couldn't remember a time when I'd needed my baby girl to laugh at one of my stupid jokes more than I did then.

"But, I can promise you something."

"What?" she replied, using her fingers to wipe the tears off her cheeks.

"I promise that I'll never just spring a woman on you. I promise, no matter what happens, you'll get a say. And I promise you'll never have to call someone else mommy."

Chapter Eleven

Grace

It had been three days since I woke up in Devon's house and made his children banana pancakes. Three days and no word from Devon at all. I hadn't expected to hear from him right away, but I could admit to myself that it hurt when three days had passed and not even a text had come through.

My mind kept wandering to the small kiss we shared. One tiny kiss. I hadn't changed my clothes, brushed my hair, or even brushed my teeth that morning, but it was one of the sweetest kisses I'd ever had. At twenty-seven, I shouldn't have been so obsessed with one kiss, but, good lord, I totally was. The way he pressed his lips almost to the corner of my mouth first, as if he were trying to make sure I wanted the kiss. It had caught me off-guard, sure, but as soon as I realized what was going on, I was all in.

So why hadn't he called? Or texted?

I had to be at work at the bar in two hours and I knew it would drive me crazy the whole time. I picked my phone up off my bedside table and decided to take the matter into my own hands, tapping away a message that showed I was concerned, but more importantly, didn't make me sound like a crazy stalker.

How's Ruby feeling?

See? I was giving him a way out, giving him the perfect opportunity to reply and tell me how sick she's been, how he'd probably be busy parenting for the foreseeable future, and then he could blow me off with a proper text message good-bye.

Minutes passed and I watched them tick by as I checked my Facebook page and even stupidly tried to get back into the book I'd been reading when I fell asleep on Devon's couch. That only resulted in having to reread the same paragraph five times.

When my phone finally buzzed in my hands, I thought for sure I was imagining it. But then the little icon showed up at the top of my screen and I lost my breath.

Hey. Ruby's doing fine now. We just kind of stayed low for a few days. But, fear not, she's back to her preteen self, attitude and all.

Okay, so it wasn't the *I'm so glad you texted me because I've been thinking about you for days* I was hoping for, but it also wasn't the *Look, you really need to get over me* I was expecting, either. It was a nice response to my question, with a little cute dad humor thrown in for good measure. Gah. Dad humor. He was a good dad. Watching him with Jax and Ruby was always endearing, but watching him take care of one of his kids was the ultimate in ovarian disruption. But now, damn him, he'd thrown the ball back in my court.

It took me a few minutes and a lot of typing and then backspacing before I was finally satisfied with my response.

I'm glad she's doing better. I've been worried.

There. Short and sweet. Not the least bit crazy stalker. It took just a minute but he responded.

Sorry I haven't called. After you left things got a little sticky with Ruby, and I'd like to talk to you about it, but not over the phone. I needed a few days with the kids. I hope you understand.

My mind immediately went back to the kitchen and Ruby asking me if I'd been on a date with her father, and suddenly I had a pretty good idea of why he'd been distant. On top of that, I felt really stupid for even thinking he owed me any kind of communication. Besides, I knew exactly what happened when you got your heart set on something and then had it taken away from you—disappointment.

Of course I understand. No explanation necessary. I'm glad she's feeling better.

And that was the coward in me texting. I regretted the message the instant I sent it. But he didn't seem fazed by it. Texting with someone you liked, especially when the relationship was new and complicated, was never a good idea. Of course, if we were talking on the phone, I'm sure there would be no way to hide the ache in my voice and he'd know I was hanging on every word, just hoarding them and tucking them away for a time when I could sit and run them through my mind over and over again.

You're working tonight, right? And all weekend, I imagine. Can I see you on Monday? Another try at dinner? Afterward there will be a surprise.

An immediate wave of sadness washed over me. How many times would we have to *try*? If there was anything my last relationship taught me, it was that trying too hard was sometimes just as destructive as not trying hard enough. Would relationships always be difficult? Would I always feel as though I had to just keep giving and giving until I had nothing left? And was I willing to give with Devon? Could I take the risk? Sign up for another dinner, another date, with "second try" written all over it?

My thumbs hovered over my phone as my mind turned in a million directions, trying to figure out what the best and least-destructive path would be. My eyes closed and I pictured Devon with his kids, the way he ruffled Jax's hair and kissed the top of Ruby's head, and my heart lurched. I remembered the way his mouth so tentatively touched mine, as though he were afraid I would break.

It was then it occurred to me, with somewhat of a jolting realization, that I wasn't fragile at all. I had lived through some of the most horrible situations— things I wouldn't wish on anyone, ever—and I was still here, pushing through each day. Devon had endured more heartbreak than I had, easily. But he was still *trying*.

I'd really like to see you again.

I sent the text message and no sooner had I pressed the button did my phone ring in my hands, showing a call from Shelby, almost as if she knew I needed someone to talk to at that exact moment.

"Your best friend ESP is on point today," I said in greeting.

"Really? That's awesome. What do you need?" I could hear her smile through the phone and it went a long way to ease the anxiety coursing through me.

"Do you remember that guy I went to Disney World with? The parent of one of my students?"

"Yeah…."

"We've seen each other a few times in the last couple weeks, but our last date went downhill fast."

"Oh, damn. What happened?"

"We went out to dinner but had to leave early because his daughter, Ruby, got sick and he had to take her to the ER. I stayed with him because he seemed like he could use the help, and I wanted to, but the whole thing was a disaster. I ended up sleeping on his couch and when Devon finally woke up, everything was awkward, until he kissed me, and then I didn't hear from him—"

"Whoa. Slow your roll, honey. Did you say Ruby and Devon?"

"Yeah," I answered, confusion apparent in my voice.

"And what was your student's name? The little boy?"

"Jax." Confusion was still sharp in my voice. "Why?"

"Are you dating Devon Roberts?"

Her question would have made me stumble backward had I been standing. "How do you know his last name? I never told you that."

"Wow. It's really ironic that your first date was at Disney because it's a small fucking world, Grace."

"What are you talking about?"

"Devon Roberts. Father to Ruby and Jax. Widower of Olivia Roberts. I knew them. Well, I knew them through Evelyn."

"You know Evelyn?" My head was beginning to hurt. "Will you just tell me what's going on?"

"I used to work with Evelyn. Do makeup and modeling for her shoots sometimes. I didn't really know Olivia or her family, except when they'd come to shows or gallery parties. But, after Olivia passed away, I spent a lot of time with Evie, working with her, but also trying to help her with the Devon situation."

"The Devon situation?" I parroted, an empty pit growing in my stomach.

"Devon and Evie went through this whole will-they-won't-they period after his wife died. From what she told me, they'd spent a lot of time throughout their entire friendship fighting an attraction, and when things got complicated between them, everything fell apart. That's when he left Fairbanks."

"Wait, Evie? His wife's best friend?"

"Yeah," she whispered.

"So, his wife died and then he started an affair with her best friend? That doesn't sound like Devon."

"It wasn't really an affair, or at least it didn't sound like one from what she told me. It was also a few years ago, so the details are fuzzy. All I know is that Evie spent a lot of time with his kids, and she eventually just kind of fell into the role left empty by Olivia. I think the lines between Devon and Evie blurred, but then it all just kind of ended. He moved and so did she."

"Wow. I had no idea. And I've met Evie. She was at Disney too. This is all so strange." I was teetering between angry that Devon hadn't told me about Evelyn, and ashamed for listening to a third-party story about him. I loved Shelby, she was my best friend, but there was no way she knew the absolute truth.

"Listen, Grace. From everything I know about him, he's a good guy. And Evie is happy with Nate. They just both went through a hard time when his wife passed and I was the person she vented to."

"Wow," I said on a breath. "What are the odds that we'd all know each other in this weird, convoluted way?"

"Like I said, it's a small, small world."

"It's just such a big coincidence. And, Shel, he hasn't told me anything about Evie, just that she and his wife were friends." I paused, trying to put my thoughts in order, and Shelby waited, just like I knew she would. "He doesn't owe me anything. We haven't even been able to complete one full date. But the connection between us…." I closed my eyes and the image of him was almost immediate. The blond hair, the blue eyes, the way his whole face would light up with a smile. "It's been so long since I felt anything for anyone. Not since Jeff. And we both know how that ended." I finished my sentence on a laugh, trying to make light of the heaviest thing in my life, the thing that weighed me down more than anything ever had or would. The proverbial boulder I felt as though I'd be pushing up a hill for eternity, just to have it roll back down and start again. "I can't go through that again."

"I know, honey," she whispered. "Maybe just talk to him. Does he know about Jeff?"

"No," I said, although it was so quiet I wasn't sure she heard me.

"I'm not saying he has to know—what you lived through is really personal and not something you need to tell everyone—but if you want anything with Devon, you're going to have to tell him eventually."

"I know. Man," I said as I sat up and ran my hand through my hair. "Dating is stupid. This whole situation is dumb. I should have started with a one-night stand. I went straight from just out of a seriously messed-up relationship to falling for a man with a lot of baggage."

"You think you're falling for him?" Shelby asked quietly.

I thought about her question, then answered honestly. "Yeah, which is why this sucks and also why I'm thinking about calling the whole thing off."

"I'm not going to tell you what to do, but I do think you should talk to him before you make any final decisions. He probably feels the same way about you, and would probably have told you about Evie eventually. And she's a really good person, too, Grace. It was a bad situation for everyone involved. Just like yours."

I knew she was right. I'd liked Evie, and in some demented way I could totally see why Devon would be attracted to her. The only way I could describe the way I felt was icky. Like I'd been left out of some joke and everyone was laughing at me—which I also knew was ridiculous.

"Thanks, Shel. Sorry to always drop all the drama on your lap."

"Hey, that's what I'm here for. And for the record, I'm pretty sure I dropped the drama on your lap this time."

"Oh, that's right. You totally did," I said with mock irritation. "But seriously, is there a reason you called? I just kind of railroaded our whole conversation."

"Not really," she replied, and I could almost hear her shrugging. "I just saw the best friend bat-signal and decided to call."

"You're the best. Thanks for always looking out for me."

"Anytime, sister."

I hung up and noticed Devon had texted me back.

Great. Will six work?*

I stared at the text and every emotion inside me waged for control. I wanted to see him, wanted to give him the benefit of the doubt, to believe that there was nothing to the story about him and Evie, but the doubt that still lingered grabbed hold tightly. If anything, I just needed a little time. Time to think clearly and work through my own issues, to come to terms with the fact that everyone had a past, even me, and that if I expected Devon to share his story with me, I should be prepared to share my own with him.

Inevitably, fear made the decision for me.

I'm sorry. I'm going to have to back out. There's a lot going on for me right now, and I think it would be best if we just took a few steps back. Maybe we can try again sometime down the line.

I sent the text, then immediately powered down my phone. I didn't want to know what Devon had to say in response. It didn't really matter. The only thing that mattered was that I didn't want to be emotionally wrecked again, and I was beginning to realize that Devon Roberts had the potential to ruin me.

I'd made it through a few hours of my shift, but I hadn't succeeded in keeping Devon from my thoughts. I wondered if he'd texted back, how he'd responded to my decision to take some time for myself, but I managed to keep my phone in my purse and not turn it on. Instead, I focused on smiling and pretending everything was fine, as I knew full well that a sulky and depressed bartender didn't make great tips.

"What time are you off tonight? Need a ride home?"

A guy who looked just barely legal had been sitting at the bar for nearly my whole shift, slowly sucking down Jack and Cokes. As was usually in the job requirement of bartenders, I made polite conversation, threw him a couple smiles, and I may have batted my eyelashes at him a few times. It was harmless flirting, and most of the time the guys played along. They didn't really want to take home the bartender, but they liked getting their egos stroked before they went out onto the wild dance floors, looking for hopefuls.

As the night went on, and the music grew louder, I was forced to lean closer to hear him order, and wasn't convinced he needed to press his lips to my ear for me to hear him, but I let it slide. Now, he was slurring his words, and sooner or later I knew I would have to tell Randy, our security, to take his keys and call him a cab.

"I don't need a ride, but even if I did, I don't think you're the right person for the job," I hollered over the loud music. I backed away, using a towel to wipe the bar, and watched as he slowly realized what I'd said, a drunken smile spreading across his face.

"I see. You like to play hard to get," he said, pointing a finger at me, eyes narrowed, as if he'd just figured me out. I just laughed and turned to another less-drunk customer to take their order. A few minutes later when I made my way down the bar again, drunken guy was gone, and I was secretly glad. I knew bartending came with its fair share of brushing off dudes, but that summer in particular seemed to be chock-full of lonely college guys looking for an easy score.

I watched as Randy passed in front of the bar, doing his security check. Every half hour he took a lap around the building while someone watched the door, just to make sure everything was on the up and up, and so people realized he was there. I'd found that just seeing Randy was the main reason he was so good at his job; no one wanted to mess with him. He was at least six foot four, easily over three hundred pounds, bald, arms full of tattoos, and had a beard that hit his chest. If you weren't afraid of him just by looking at him, you were stupid. The funny part was, he was a big softy. I'd caught the tail end of a phone conversation in

Anie Michaels | 109

which he was talking to his granddaughter about Barbie, and ever since he told her that the purple shoes went better with the silver dress than the pink, I knew there was a gooey center to him.

He nodded as he passed me by, and I nodded back, which was our code for "Everything here is fine." Had he passed by when drunk guy was still hitting on me, I would have flagged him down. He made his way through the dance floor and up onto the DJ's stage without incident. I watched as Randy's eyes roamed over the crowd, looking for any sign of drunken frat boy shenanigans. When he seemed satisfied that no one was going to cause any problems, he made his way back to the front door, where he acted as bouncer and general scarer of the clientele.

Roxanne, the other girl working the bar that night, slid over to my side and leaned toward me.

"I'm gonna take my break and then cover you while you take yours, all right? I just served up everyone on my side, so they should be good for a few."

"Got it," I said, nodding. "Have a good break." She smiled and then disappeared toward the back where I knew she would sit on a chair, drinking Diet Coke, and text her boyfriend for all fifteen minutes of her break.

I ran my tail off while she was gone, making my way from one end of the bar all the way to the other, making sure everyone got what they needed. The crowd was a little rowdier than usual, but as the summer wore on, it was to be expected.

When Roxanne returned, she was all smiles, so I figured her boyfriend had texted all the right emojis.

"I got this, Grace. Go ahead and take your break," she said, still smiling.

"Thanks," I said, placing my hand on her shoulder as I passed her and walked right into the break room. I never stayed in the building for my breaks, but instead took the opportunity to rest my eardrums. I grabbed the light jacket I'd brought with me and then headed out the back door.

There was a designated area for employees to smoke out back, but since it was late, there usually wasn't more than one person on break at a time. I pulled up a crate and took a seat, letting out a large sigh, relishing the relative quiet.

It was disturbed by a drunken voice that came from nowhere.

"Here you are. I couldn't find you at the bar, so I went lookin'. An' here you are."

I looked up to see drunken frat boy wobbling toward me.

Great. I hated dealing with the drunk college kids, and I definitely didn't have the patience that night.

"Hey, what are you doing back here?" I stood up and took a step toward him, only to watch him stumble and almost hit the ground. I reached out quickly, catching his arm. "Whoa there, you all right? I think we need to go back up front and get Randy to call you a cab."

"Only if you're coming home with me," he said, clumsily pushing me back against the building. The rough brick of the wall bit into my back where my shirt didn't quite meet my pants. I tried to push him off, but even drunk he was stronger than me. His hands pinned my arms against the wall, just below my shoulders.

"Let me go," I said forcefully, hoping that if I couldn't pry my arms free, perhaps I could use my voice to intimidate him. I tried to pull free again, but all

I accomplished was scraping my arms along the brick wall.

"Not so fast," he said, moving his face closer to mine, the alcohol on his breath making bile rise in my throat. "You're a tease." His words were whispered but filled with anger. "You were practically begging me to take you home in there, and then you went all cold on me. How do I know you're not playing hard to get now?" His face was moving closer with his words; there was now barely any space between us.

Before he could say any more crazy words, I drew in a deep breath and took the one shot I wasn't even sure I had. I pulled my knee up as hard and fast as I could, and made contact right between his legs.

Drunken frat boy fell to the ground, groaning and clutching his crotch.

"Grace?" I turned to see Devon standing at the edge of the building, eyes bouncing between me and drunk guy on the ground.

"Devon?"

"Are you all right?" he asked, running over to me. "I went in the bar looking for you, but they said you were out back." He glanced down, watching as drunken frat boy rolled from side to side. "Did you do this?"

My mind was whirling around, ricocheting from the scary feeling of being held against my will to the relief of putting the man to the ground, then to the shock and surprise of seeing Devon.

"What's going on back here?" My eyes went to Randy, and even more relief flooded through me.

"This guy attacked me," I said on a sigh, pushing the hair from my forehead, then leaning back against the wall, suddenly feeling very weak.

Drunken frat boy groaned again from the ground, then said, "You bitch."

"All right, buddy, time to take a ride to the drunk tank." Randy came over to the guy, rolled him to his stomach, and then pressed his knee into his back, winning another grunt from him. Randy then whipped out his cell and I heard him giving our location to—I assumed—the 911 operator.

"You all right?" Devon asked, coming to stand right in front of me, his hands cupping the sides of my face. He was exactly where drunken frat boy had been just one minute earlier, but his presence didn't scare me. In fact, it soothed me. I leaned forward until my head rested against his chest and sighed as his hands slid around me, bringing me closer.

"I'm okay," I said, shivering as I spoke the words. He pulled me even closer still, running his hands up and down my back. "I sure am glad you showed up when you did."

He let out a deep sigh, then said, "Looks like you laid him out all on your own."

"Yeah," I said, trying to fight the tears that were welling in my eyes. I was feeling so much, and it was all boiling over.

"Hey, you're all right. I'm right here." At his words, I pressed in closer. When I saw red and blue lights flashing around us, I looked up. Then I heard Randy's voice.

"Hey, lookie here, scumbag. Your ride showed up." The guy struggled beneath him, but it was useless. The two cops hopped out of their cars and took over wrangling the drunk guy. They got him cuffed and then put him in the back of the vehicle. One cop focused his attention on drunken frat boy, and the other came over to me, notepad open. Randy stood watch over me, which I appreciated, but Devon never left my side, his hand running smoothly up and down my back as I recounted to the officer what had happened.

"I'm not sure what he was planning on doing with me, if anything, but I just reacted on instinct and kneed him. He fell to the ground and then Randy and Devon showed up."

"He's lucky you got to him before I could," Devon said quietly.

"I reckon he is," the police officer replied, not looking up from his notepad.

"I'm actually kind of sad I didn't get a go at him," Randy added, eliciting a laugh from the cop.

"So, here's the deal. We'll take him to the station and book him, let him dry out. It's up to you if you want to press charges. At the very least you should get a restraining order, just to keep him from coming back here and bothering you. But the decision is yours. Since all we have is him physically assaulting you, that's all the charge would be, even though we're not sure what he was planning."

"Do I have to decide now?"

"No, ma'am. You've got two years to press charges, but the longer you wait, the less likely the charges are to stick. If you want him charged, I wouldn't wait more than forty-eight hours."

"Okay."

He flipped his notepad closed, but pulled a card out of a pocket in the front cover and handed it to me. "If you have any more information, feel free to call or e-mail me. He'll be locked up for at least twenty-four hours."

"Thank you," I said, gingerly taking the card, then looked down at my body, realizing I had nowhere to put it. Devon slowly reached out and took the card from me, putting it in his wallet.

"You go on home, Grace. If you need tomorrow off, just give us a call," Randy said softly, the smoothest I've ever heard his voice. "Take all the time you need."

I nodded and tried to speak, but my words were breathy and had no sound. I was balancing on the edge of a breakdown, so I just kept nodding.

"Let's go, baby," Devon said, wrapping an arm around my shoulders, guiding me toward the front of the building where the parking lot was located.

"I need my purse," I said suddenly, remembering it was still in my locker in the break room.

"I got it, Grace," Randy said, disappearing into the bar.

I followed along with Devon, stopping when he came to the passenger side of his SUV. He opened the door and I climbed in without words or arguments. Randy brought him my purse and Devon climbed in, started the engine, and pulled out of the parking lot. I leaned my head against the window, watching the street lights pass by, and didn't realize he'd driven me home until he parked the car.

"Hey, you okay?" he asked, turning the car off.

"Yeah," I said, even though I wasn't sure. "Thank you for the ride," I said as I unbuckled my seat belt.

"You're welcome, but I'm not just dropping you off."

"What do you mean?"

"You don't really think I'm going to let you stay alone in your apartment the night some guy attacks you, do you?"

"You're... staying?"

"Do you want me to go?"

It took me a moment, but I slowly shook my head. "No, I don't."

With that, he opened his door and came around to open mine. "Keys?" he said, holding his hand out. I dug them out of my purse and handed them over. He took them, then reached his other hand out to me and I took it. He led me to my door, opened it, then let me go in first. I took a few steps in and toed off my shoes, a little unsure of what came next. I didn't want to be alone, necessarily, but Devon was the last person I'd expected to see that night.

"What can I do for you?" he asked gently, coming up right behind me, running his hands down my bare arms. His soft touch smoothed over the same spot that was now tender from the strong grip of drunken frat boy, and I pulled away before I could think not to. "Do you want to take a bath? Watch a movie? Read a book? What do you want?"

I took a few more steps inside, placing my jacket over one of my dining room chairs. I took in a deep breath, then let it out, my mind empty and racing all at the same time. The only thing I could think of was turning off my brain. "I just want to go to sleep."

Devon held my gaze for a few moments, then stepped toward me, closing the distance. One hand came to the back of my head and pulled me in as he pressed his lips to my forehead.

"I'll be here if you need me." He said the words against my hair and I could almost feel them burrowing into my heart, making their place permanent there.

I twisted my fingers in the cloth of his T-shirt, holding him as close to me as possible. "Will you do me a favor?" I asked, too embarrassed by my request to look him in the eye.

"Anything," he said earnestly.

"Come to bed with me." I felt his breathing halt at my words, the rhythmic movements of his chest stopping, then starting up again. He pulled back and I let him go, expecting him to make some excuse to leave, but all he did was slip his shoes off, leaving them next to mine. He took my hand and led me back to my bedroom. He didn't bother turning on the light, just walked to my bed and crawled in. He scooted all the way over to the other side, then held the blankets up in invitation.

I didn't even think twice about it.

I climbed into the bed, lined my body up with his as he tucked the blankets around us, and sighed as I felt myself relaxing against him. His hand came up to stroke my hair, and his lips touched the side of my head.

"Sleep now," he whispered.

So I did.

Chapter Twelve

Devon

I woke up before the sun streamed into the window and I selfishly took the opportunity to watch Grace sleep. She was beautiful, but she was troubled. Every few minutes the soft skin between her eyebrows would bunch up and I knew she was dreaming. I could only hope she wouldn't remember the dreams when she woke up.

Eventually I slid out from under her, successfully trying not to wake her, and slipped into the bathroom.

When I walked back into the bedroom, I was shocked by her beauty. I shouldn't have been; I knew how beautiful she was. But I'd never seen her so beautiful or vulnerable before. She was still asleep, on her stomach, her arms wrapped around the pillow beneath her head. Her hair was everywhere and her face was relaxed, the worry lines gone.

The image of her the night before, her body pressed up against a brick wall, fear in her wide eyes, flashed in my mind. It didn't take a rocket scientist to figure out what had happened, and all I'd wanted to do when I saw him on the ground was beat the shit out of him. The only thing that stopped me was the look on Grace's face—a look that said she'd had enough, that said she needed someone to support her in that moment, not avenge her. My need to comfort her took over, but I knew if I ever saw him again, he'd need an ambulance to take him away when I was through.

She was still in her clothes from work, and I was still in my jeans and T-shirt, but we'd slept all night that way. I pulled my phone from my pocket, checking to make sure there weren't any messages, then I placed it on the bedside table and climbed gently back in the bed, trying again not to disturb her. I curled my body around hers, softly draping my arms over her waist, pulling her into me.

I didn't know if she wanted me to sleep with her to make her feel safe, or just to keep her mind off what had happened, but there was no denying I felt a fuck of a lot better having her in my arms.

I knew there hadn't been a chance of me leaving her alone the night before. I was fully prepared to sleep on her couch; sharing her bed had never even crossed my mind. But when she asked me to go to bed with her, I didn't stand a chance. Not that I wanted to.

I faded away again, listening to her slow breaths.

"Devon."

The soft whispers pulled me from sleep. Halfway between sleep and consciousness I felt the featherlight touches on my skin. Before I opened my eyes, I knew Grace was running her fingertip over my face.

"Devon, wake up," she whispered again, and I could feel her breath on my chin. Then the minty smell hit me.

"I'm awake," I mumbled.

"Where are the kids?" she asked urgently.

"With my mom," I grumbled, then I shot my arms out, wrapped them around her, and pulled her into me, burrowing my face in her wild hair. "Go back to sleep."

"I'm not tired anymore." Her voice held an edge of laughter, and damn, I wanted to hear that. Especially after what happened the night before. If she was ready to laugh, I was prepared to be the one to make it happen. I flipped her over so her back was to me again, and pulled her to me, leaving absolutely no space between us. I rested my hand on her waist, giving her a tiny squeeze, and everything inside me lit up when I heard her laughter. "No tickling!" She was shrieking and laughing, trying to wiggle her way out of my arms.

Finally, when she was out of breath and smiling, I stopped, but still held her close. Her breathing slowed, and every few moments a rogue giggle slipped out of her, but she didn't try to pull away or make me let her go. She relaxed into me, running her fingers softly up and down my arm.

"Devon?" she finally asked.

"Yeah?"

"Why were you at the bar last night?"

I let out a sigh. I'd known this part of the conversation was coming, I had just originally thought we would have had it the night before. Grace rolled so she was facing me, but put a little distance between us. I wanted to reach out and obliterate it, but I let her have her space.

"You blew me off, and I wasn't prepared to let you go. So I went to find you." I said the words as though they were evident. Self-explanatory. And to me, they were. She'd pushed me away without a reason, and I wasn't prepared to take no for an answer. "Somewhere along the line, something got between us, and I'm not sure what it was. But I was sure that if I could talk to you last night, I could make it go away."

I reached out and tucked away a piece of her hair, gently looping it behind her ear, never breaking eye contact. Her hair was impossibly soft and I wanted to thread my fingers through it, feel it slip between them.

"I knew you'd be at work, and I remembered the name of the bar, so I asked my mom to watch the kids overnight and I went looking for you."

I watched her eyes change, watched her retreat back into her mind, insecurity painting her face.

"Hey," I said, bringing my hand to her cheek, trying to get her to look back at me. "Don't run away from me. I'm right here. What happened between those two text messages that changed your mind about us?" Her eyes met mine again, but her teeth were worrying her lip and her eyes still looked unsure. I trailed my thumb down her cheekbone, trying to coax the words from her. Finally, she spoke.

"I moved to Fairbanks with my husband right after we graduated. We agreed we'd go wherever the first job offer came from. Jeff got an offer first, and I was a substitute teacher for a few years before I got my job. During the first summer we were there I took a job as a receptionist at a salon. Shelby, my best friend since middle school, had just graduated from the beautician academy and I got her a job where I worked. She made a good name for herself and started doing makeup jobs outside of the salon."

Grace grew quiet, as if she were contemplating the next part of her story, and I couldn't figure out how any of it had anything to do with us.

"Since Shelby is also a model, she did some work with local photographers. Turns out, she worked with Evie and they were also friends. Still are, in fact."

I had to admit, that information caught me off guard, but it still didn't give me the insight I was looking for.

"Anyway, she just happened to call yesterday while you and I were texting and we got to talking, and she eventually figured out that the Devon I was dating was the same Devon her friend Evie had been, um, involved with."

Slowly the pieces were falling into place, and the light was growing brighter and brighter in my mind. Her eyes fell away from me again, to look down at her hands, which were fiddling with some imaginary piece of lint. I watched her turn back inward.

"Grace," I said, wanting to physically take her face in my hands and make her look at me, and only stopping myself because I knew she was in defense mode. "I don't know what Shelby told you, but Evie and I were never together."

"I know," she whispered, but as soon as the words were out of her mouth her eyes snapped up to meet mine. "Actually, I don't know, because *you* didn't tell me. And that's what really bothered me." Her eyes darted back and forth between mine and it looked as though she were gathering her courage, like she was building up some sort of strength. It was both exhilarating and terrifying to watch, because I knew whatever she had coming, she was aiming for me. "Listen, my ex-husband did a number on me, and in the end I looked like a fool. The last thing I wanted was to go through that again. So yes, anger was my first reaction to learning that you'd had some sort of romantic *thing* happening with the woman I'd spent a day at Disney befriending. The woman who is like an aunt to your kids. And listen," she said, holding up a hand in front of my face when I tried to interject. "I like Evie, I can see why you'd be attracted to her, not to mention she's one of the sweetest people I've ever met. So I can't blame you there. It just made me feel really foolish not to know. Like it was a big joke everyone was in on, except for me."

122 | The Presence of Grace

At that point I did reach out and gently take her face in my hands, scooting closer and looking her in the eye.

"The last thing I ever want to do is make you feel anything but happy." My words earned me the tiniest smile, but I couldn't stop. I had to keep going. "I would have told you about Evie eventually, but Disney didn't seem like the time or place. And since then, well, every time we've been together something has happened. But, *believe me*, I would have told you. I wasn't trying to keep you in the dark." I paused, sweeping both my thumbs over her cheeks. "Evie isn't a dark secret. She's not something to tuck away. She's important to me and to my kids. But, Grace, you don't have to worry about my relationship with her."

"Will you tell me about her?" she asked shyly, her voice nothing but a whisper.

"Yes, of course. I'll tell you anything." I took a breath, trying to mentally put all the pieces of Evie and me together in the correct order. There were so many edges of us that never fit just right together, nothing like Grace and me. We relaxed back onto our own sides of the bed, and she looked at me expectantly, begging me with her eyes not to hurt her. "I met Evie one day in college. Some guy bumped into her and soaked her shirt, so I gave her mine. We were young and, sure, there was an attraction there, but we both went our separate ways. A week later I met Olivia. A few weeks after, Olivia and I were already together and I realized her best friend was Evie. Evie and I both knew we'd been attracted to each other. It was a strange situation, to say the least, but the pull to Olivia, for me, was bigger than my attraction to Evie. There was never any question that I would be faithful to her." I took another deep breath. I knew the hardest part of the story was coming, and I wanted to make her realize that even though my past with Evie was complicated and messy, our relationship now was simple, easy, and completely platonic.

"But after Olivia passed away, Evie and I fell into a new sort of relationship. She was there for me, there to help with the kids, and she made everything easier. I'll admit I used her to put off dealing with Olivia's death. Evie was there and she'd stepped right into Olivia's role. She didn't do it on purpose, she wasn't trying to take her place, she was just trying to help." I ran my hand down my face, bracing myself for the worst part of the story.

"You can tell me," Grace whispered. I looked at her and saw wide eyes staring back. She looked open, and I felt as though I could tell her anything. And then, more than ever, I *needed* to tell her. I needed her to know everything so that whatever we had, whatever could grow between us, had a fighting chance.

"One night, I came home from work, and I don't know what I was thinking, but I saw her there and my instincts took over. I went to her, wrapped my arm around her, then I think I might have kissed her on the cheek. The point was, I'm sure part of me thought it was Liv, like there'd been some miracle and my wife was standing in the kitchen making dinner just like she had for so many years. But there was definitely a part of me that knew it was Evie and wanted her, if only for just a moment."

"Okay," Grace said, accepting every single thing I was saying as if I were explaining how to change the oil on her car.

"No, it wasn't okay. None of it was. We'd spent, shit, I don't know, ten years dancing around this strange attraction we'd had to one another, and when I lost my wife I lost the ability to make rational decisions and I fucked it up with Evie. I didn't fuck a relationship up with her, because looking back on it, it never would have worked between us, but I fucked up our friendship. She was so vulnerable. We both were. And we did things we shouldn't have. We kissed. Once. And it was important, but only because it wasn't. Evie and I will never be together. If we had spent a little time actually figuring that out, we wouldn't have spent ten years wondering. Does that make sense?"

"Not even a little bit."

I dropped my head on the pillow, frustration seeping out of me.

"I've told you everything that happened. All the important stuff, anyway. But there's one more thing. I never cheated on Olivia. Not once. But I did spend a lot of time wondering what my life would have been like if I'd chosen Evie instead. And that's the God's honest truth. It wasn't fair to Olivia and it wasn't fair to Evie, either. I see that now. I *learned* that. So, I need you to understand that I will never, *never*, spend time with another woman unless I'm completely sure she's the only one for me."

"Okay," she said again.

"It's you, Grace," I said, wrapping my arm around her waist, pulling her to my side of the bed, pressing her body against mine. "It's you. No one else," I whispered, my eyes taking in all of her face, trying to figure out what she was thinking by the clues in her eyes. But then my gaze landed on her lips and only one thought pounded through my head. "I'm going to kiss you. If you don't want me to, you're going to have to tell me."

"Okay," she whispered.

When it was obvious she wasn't going to stop me, I inched forward, my lips coming softly into contact with hers. This was no banana pancake kiss; that had been spur of the moment, a kiss so quick it was over before I really knew it happened. This kiss, it was purposeful and a long time coming.

I moved my hand slowly up her cheek, then slipped behind her neck, pulling her closer, wanting her as close as possible. Her hands gripped my shirt, her fingers twisting in the material as a soft moan slipped through her lips.

My tongue gently touched her lips, asking, and when she opened for me, it was as if every tether I'd felt in the last few years had been snapped. There was nothing holding me back any longer. I angled my mouth over hers and rolled us so she was beneath me. She was with me, her fingertips finding the hem of my shirt and gliding up my torso, her knees spreading to accommodate me, then lifting to bring me into her tighter.

For over three years I'd wondered what it would feel like to be with a woman again, to feel a warm body below me, to be consumed by the scent of someone other than my wife. Grace felt nothing like Olivia. She was different and new and fantastic. The guilt I thought I would feel was absent, the longing for something I'd never have again not even a thought in my mind. What I was thinking about was how soft Grace's lips were, how wonderful it felt when she used her ankle to anchor me to her, to hold me to her as though letting me go was the worst thing that could happen.

What I wasn't prepared for were the teenage-like hormones running through me. I hadn't *needed* anyone in a very long time, but I needed Grace. *God*, I needed her. With one forearm braced on the bed, my free hand found her waist, squeezing as I went, wanting to feel all of her. From her waist my hand traveled south, over her hip and around to her ass. I palmed her there, my fingers digging in to the jeans that covered her flesh, groaning as she wrapped her arms around me.

"Devon," she said, her voice gravelly and rough, turning her mouth away from mine, but giving me unfettered access to her throat.

"Hmmm." I hummed against the skin of her neck, unwilling to disconnect. My lips and tongue worshiped her there, my teeth nipping slightly, eliciting a rough and sharp inhalation from her.

"It's been a while…," she started, but then ended on a moan as I found a spot behind her ear she seemed to be particularly fond of. "Since I've… oh, God…."

I couldn't help but smirk against her, loving the fact that I was scrambling her thoughts with my mouth.

"It's just, I'm not sure I'm ready…." Her words trailed away again, but I got the impression it was less about me and more about her. She wasn't ready. So even though it would pain me later, I pulled away, immediately finding her eyes with my own.

"I'm sorry," she whispered immediately. "You being here was the last thing I expected, and I hadn't planned on you, and even though my body is really enjoying what you're doing to it, my brain is really insistent that we slow down."

"You don't have to apologize, Grace. But can I ask you a question?"

"Sure," she breathed.

"What is your heart insisting on?"

She blinked up at me, nothing but patience and vulnerability. "It's begging me not to let you break it."

I looked at her for a moment, not sure I'd ever had anyone speak words to me that were so completely full of truth and fear and hope. Then I leaned down and kissed her again, only that time it was slow and soft.

An hour later, after Grace had showered and changed and we'd stopped for coffee, I was driving her back to the bar to get her car.

"Have you thought about whether you're going to press charges?" I asked softly. The last thing I wanted to do was upset her.

"I haven't decided yet." She ran her hand through her chocolate-colored hair that was down and drying against her shoulders. "I've seen guys like him a lot, being behind a bar. He seemed harmless, and I took him down easily enough when it came down to it. Part of me thinks he was just overconfident, you know? The booze made him bold. He's just a kid, and I hate the idea of potentially ruining his life over one mistake. But, then I think about what if he tries it with someone else? What if she can't fight him off as easily? I'm not sure I could live with myself if he hurt someone else because I let him off the hook."

The more she spoke, the more I wanted just five minutes alone with the dickhead. I also wanted to lock Ruby up in a tower. Or enroll her in Krav Maga classes. Or both. I reached over and took her hand, pulling it into my lap and running my thumb over the back.

"I'll stand behind whatever decision you make, but you have to remember that you're not responsible for his actions. Not last night and not tomorrow. Or next month. If you decide not to press charges, you can't worry about every female in Florida."

"Thanks," she said, trying to smile, but it was obvious her thoughts were still plaguing her.

I pulled into the parking spot next to her car, put my car in Park, then turned my body to face her.

"Hey," I said, using one hand to bring her face around, looking into her blue eyes. "You going to be all right?"

"Yeah," she answered softly, but then continued, her voice a little stronger. "Thanks to you."

"I didn't do anything." I ran my thumb over the roundness of her cheek.

"Yeah, you did." Her voice just a whisper again. "You came back for me, you protected me, you took care of me, you were honest with me, and you respected me."

"Well." I smiled. "When you put it that way." Her mouth tipped up into a smile and it felt like the sun had just come out and peeked over a dark horizon. She was so beautiful. "Come over for dinner tonight. The kids will be home, I'll cook, it'll be really low-key."

"Okay," she agreed without a second of hesitation. "I'll have to leave early to go to work, though."

"No problem, we'll eat early. How's five?"

"Sounds great." Her smile grew wider and I couldn't stop myself from leaning over the console and kissing her, letting my fingers tangle in the wet strands of her hair.

When I finally pulled away, it was only because I knew she had things to do; I would have gladly stayed there and kissed her all day. But instead, she smiled at me again and then I watched as she opened her car door, got inside, and backed out of her parking spot.

It gave me a little relief to know she was safely on her way home, but then I shook off the image of her in the back of the building the night before, fighting off that douche bag. My fingers tightened on the steering wheel, knuckles turning white. I hated the idea of her in a bar four nights a week with drunken assholes, but I also knew it wasn't my place to tell her to quit or ask her to look for something different. Something safer.

I let out a breath, shaking out my hands, then aimed my SUV toward my parents' house to pick up my kids.

Hours later, Jaxy was playing Minecraft in the living room and Ruby was lying on the couch next to him reading a book. They'd both been surprisingly quiet and well-behaved all day, which I wasn't going to complain about.

"Hey, kiddos, scootch." Ruby swung her legs around, making room for me on the couch next to her. "Jaxy, eyes for a minute." I waited for the groan or eye rolling, but he didn't even grumble, just put the controller down and turned to look at me. "So, I wanted to talk to you guys about something."

Ruby folded down the top corner of the page of her book, closed it, then looked at me with eyes that were exact replicas of her mother's.

I swallowed hard, trying to find the words I'd been practicing in my head all day since I picked them up. "I want to talk to you guys about Grace." This piqued Ruby's interest, her eyebrows shooting up, but Jax just looked attentive, waiting for my next words. "I've invited her over for dinner tonight, and I wanted to talk to you about it."

"I like Grace," Jaxy said matter-of-factly. "I don't care if she comes to dinner."

"Jax, Daddy's talking to us because he wants to *date* Grace, not just have her over for dinner."

"What does that mean?" he asked his sister, all his eight-year-old innocence showing through.

"It means Daddy wants Grace to be his girlfriend and he wants us to be okay with it."

I watched as his eyebrows drew close together, crinkling in the middle, thoughts obviously running through his mind.

"So, he's going to hold her hand and kiss her and stuff?"

"Yeah," Ruby answered. "And she'll probably be over here a lot, and Daddy will be taking us to Grandma and Grandpa's more, since they'll want to go out on dates."

"Grandma gives us cookies every time we go to her house!" Jaxy exclaimed, all too excited by the promise of sugar. His eyes turned to me, a huge sneaky grin across his face. "You can go on as many dates with Grace as you want, Daddy. We don't mind."

My eyes darted between my two children. Had Ruby just given Jax the deep and meaningful "Daddy's Going to Date Again" speech I'd been dreading all day? I knew Ruby was a little more clued in to what was happening between Grace and me, but I expected a little more of a reaction from Jax. Who was I to argue with the logic of cookies at Grandma's house? My mom's cookies were phenomenal.

"It's not just cookies, Jax," I replied softly, wanting to make sure he understood as much as an eight-year-old could. "I'm spending time with Grace because I care about her, and I want everyone to be comfortable. Does that make sense?"

Jaxy shrugged. "I know you care about her. She's really nice." At this point it became obvious Jaxy thought I was being ridiculous, his tone indicating that he already knew everything I was trying to tell him.

"So, you're okay if we see more of her and she spends time with us?"

"Sure," he answered, shrugging again. I reached out and ruffled his hair. He ducked away from me, laughing, then turned his attention back to his video game. It seemed as though I'd been worrying myself over nothing. And that was good; I was glad the kids seemed all right with Grace and me spending time together, but it didn't mean that further down the line things might still get tricky. This was only the first hurdle, but I was glad it was over.

"What are you making for dinner?" Ruby asked.

"Huh?" Her question pulled me from the thoughts bouncing around inside my mind.

"Dinner? With Grace? What are you making?"

"I was just planning on grilling."

Ruby rolled her eyes and let out an exasperated sigh.

"What?" I asked, laughing at her complete and utter annoyance.

"You always grill when someone comes to dinner."

I shrugged. "I'm good at it." That was the truth—I *was* good at it. But more importantly, it was something I knew I couldn't mess up. It was easy and simple, but tasted damn good.

"But it would be more impressive if you made an effort."

Well, damn.

"When did you get so smart?"

Another roll of Ruby's eyes made me laugh.

"Come on, Jax. Daddy's got to go to the store. We're going to make something delicious for dinner."

Chapter Thirteen

Grace

I knocked on Devon's door and tried to ignore the flurry of nervous butterflies swarming in my belly. When the door flew open, it was Jax's smile that greeted me, and that went a long way to ease my anxiousness.

"Hi, Grace. Come on in. Daddy's in the kitchen with Ruby."

"Thank you," I said as I stepped into the house, unable to keep the smile from my face.

"Dad," Jax yelled, even though the kitchen wasn't very far away. "Grace is here!"

I was still laughing as I walked around the corner and into the open dining room between the kitchen and living room.

"Hi," Devon said, looking up at me hurriedly. "You're early."

"Am I?" Quickly pulling my phone from my purse and glancing at the time, I gave him a puzzled look. "It's five till. You said five o'clock, right?"

"Yeah," he said, his eyes not on me anymore, but on whatever he was working on in the kitchen instead. "I thought I had five more minutes." He said the words, then glanced at me, giving me a flirty wink.

"Dad," Ruby said, her tone admonishing, then popped up beside her father. "That's no way to make Grace feel welcome."

"They've been in there all afternoon. Dad's making dinner and Ruby's making dessert."

"Oh?"

"Yeah. We spent, like, an hour at the grocery store." Jax groaned as he said the words, as if the grocery store was the worst way he could have spent sixty minutes.

Before I could respond I felt a hand at my shoulder and when I turned, Devon was there.

"Sorry," he said, just before pressing a soft kiss to my cheek. When he pulled back he was wearing his sexy smile, making a shiver run down my spine. "I'm glad you're here."

"Jax claims you've been busy."

"Ah, yes." His hand slid down from my shoulder to the small of my back, leading me forward. The closer I got to the kitchen, the more I could smell what they were cooking.

"Daddy was going to grill for you, but I told him that was a terrible idea for a date." Ruby spoke while all her attention was on whatever she had pulled out of the oven moments ago. I raised my eyebrows and looked at Devon. He noticed my puzzled look and leaned in to whisper in my ear.

"I had the dating conversation with them earlier today. Everyone's on board."

"Oh," I said, even more surprised by his sentence than Ruby's mention of the word date. I wanted the kids to be comfortable with Devon and me together, but I'd thought that would come with time. I assumed we'd be easing into everything, giving them time to adjust. Apparently, the Roberts clan was more of a rip-the-Band-Aid-off kind of family. The kind of people who jumped in the pool without testing the temperature first. "Uh, grilling would have been fine," I stammered, trying to cover for the fact that ever since I walked in the door it was one surprise after another.

"No," Devon said softly, "Ruby's right. I'll grill for you some other time. But tonight I shall dazzle you with all the culinary expertise three hours and YouTube have earned me."

I lifted one eyebrow. "Is it too late to claim I'm ill?"

"None of that," he said, laughing. "Ruby has helped a lot. I'm sure it's edible. Well, mostly sure."

"It smells amazing, whatever it is."

Devon gave me another smile, then turned to Jax. "Buddy, take Grace's things and put them on my bed, okay?"

"All right," he said, holding his arms out toward me like a stiff little robot. All I had was my purse so I placed it in his hands and watched with a smile as he dutifully marched it back to Devon's bedroom.

"Would you like some wine?"

"Sure, I think one glass would be fine before work."

"I think white goes with the meal better. Is that all right?" He peered at me over the top of the refrigerator door, and I was stunned for a moment by the effort he was putting forth. I'd thought I was coming over for dinner, something casual and light, and while nothing felt heavy, I was shocked by the time and attention Devon and his children had put into this one meal.

"White would be lovely."

"I wanted to make chocolate lava cakes, but I needed to make sure they would turn out all right, so I made just one first. Kind of like a test cake," Ruby said as she grabbed a fork. "If I did this correctly and followed the recipe right, when I cut into this cake, hot chocolate sauce should pour out of it like a volcano." She looked determined, but also a little nervous to cut into the small round cake, but she finally sliced into it with her fork. She let out an excited cry as the chocolate sauce poured out of the cake. "I did it!" She bounced up and down on her feet while putting the one bite of cake in her mouth. "And it tastes good," she said, the words muffled slightly by the dessert.

"That's impressive, Ruby."

She gave me a proud smile.

"She really wanted to make something fancy for dessert. I was just going to buy a cheesecake or something, but she wouldn't let me."

I watched as I tried to hide a grin as Ruby rolled her eyes. "Men," she said with a sigh.

"All right," Devon said, giving Ruby a soft and playful flick on the tip of her nose. "Go make sure the table is all set." She walked out of the kitchen just as Devon handed me a glass of wine. "I've put together for you a creamy broccoli, bacon, and chicken pasta."

My eyes widened at his words. "You have?"

"Yes, and I know I'm the one who made it, but it looks delicious. And the good news is, it was easy to make so if it tastes as good as it looks, my kids and I thank you for the new meal in our rotation. Pizza, burgers, and hot dogs were getting a little old." He took a sip of his own wine, and then led me to the table, which was set with mismatched plates and cups with paper napkins folded underneath the silverware. The effort he went to for dinner didn't go unnoticed, but it was also endearing that it was still a glaringly bachelor setup. He led me to one end of the rectangular table and pulled out a chair for me, pushing it in as I sat. Before I realized what was happening, he placed a kiss on the side of my neck. My breath caught in my throat, and then a shiver shot down my spine as he spoke against the sensitive skin of my neck. "You smell amazing."

Oh, man. My body was emblazoned just by one kiss and a few sweet words.

I felt the heat of his body move away and watched as he went back into the kitchen. I took another sip of my wine, trying to convince my body that it wasn't, in fact, on fire.

"Ruby, Jax, come to the table," Devon hollered.

The next forty-five minutes were surreal. Most of the time I felt like an outsider, watching from the other side of a window, peering into a manifestation of every dream I'd ever had as a woman. Then there were other times, instances when Devon or one of the kids spoke to me, where I wanted to pinch myself just as a reminder that this wasn't my reality.

Ruby and Jax bickered and argued. Devon scolded. Then he joked and the kids laughed. They talked about their days, what was exciting and what was disappointing. They made plans. They smiled. The kids told stories about their dad in an effort to embarrass him, and sometimes succeeded. Devon blushed and told the children he had much more embarrassing stories about them he could tell if they didn't stop. The children laughed at his threat and then he gave me a bashful smile.

I was circling the emotional drain, swirling around and hitting every emotional checkpoint on the way down. I was laughing with them one minute and then trying to hold back tears the next, taking sips of wine to try and hide the sudden sadness and panic that came on with the wave of devastation.

This.

This was what I'd always wanted. A family. To sit around a table with a man and children, but in my dreams, those children were mine and the man belonged to me as well. There was something about witnessing the normalcy of life between Devon and his children that sent me reeling.

He was a father, and I'd never be a mother. This gaping difference between us hadn't occurred to me before sitting at a dinner table with the evidence. Well, that wasn't true. I'd known all along Devon had children; what I hadn't anticipated was how dating a man with children would make me feel. I'd pictured the rest of my life childless—the only children being the ones I taught and sent home at the end of the day. I'd always imagined dating a man with children would be too difficult, too close to the gaping wound that was always festering, and I was beginning to see that I was perhaps not capable of watching a man father his children without being constantly reminded that I'd never be given the opportunity to parent.

But then he'd look at me over his wine glass, eyes blazing, lips smiling, and something inside me would shift and crumble, just melt away with the heat of his gaze, and the idea of *not* being with him was suddenly the greater of two evils.

Dinner was over but Ruby needed fifteen minutes to bake a new batch of lava cakes, so Devon led me out to his patio. He shut the sliding door behind us, effectively blocking out the noise of Ruby and Jax bickering in the kitchen. I walked to the edge of the deck, resting my wine glass on the railing, and smiled when I felt Devon's front hit my back. He pressed in close, resting his hands on the deck, caging me in. I loved it. Loved feeling enveloped by him, surrounded and protected.

"I'm glad you came to dinner tonight," he whispered, his words a breath against my neck, sending shivers throughout my body.

"Me too. Dinner was delicious."

"It's funny because when I pictured myself dating again, I imagined it being so much harder than this. I thought there would be a problem with Ruby, mostly, having a hard time with another woman coming into the picture."

"You didn't think Jax would object?"

I both heard and felt Devon's deep intake of breath, and the sigh that immediately followed.

"I wasn't sure how he'd react, honestly—it could have gone either way. The truth of the matter is, Jaxy doesn't really remember Olivia much. When she first passed he missed her, of course, but kids are resilient and he just kept trucking along. But the older he gets the fuzzier his early memories become. And that's all he had—early memories. Ruby remembers more, which is why I thought she'd have a harder time. She remembers her mother and father together." He paused for a moment and pressed a small kiss against the side of my neck. "I think the easiness has more to do with you than anything."

"Me?"

"Yeah, you," he said, laughing, his lips still pressed against my throat. "Jaxy obviously already knew he liked you, and Ruby fell right in line. It wouldn't have been this easy with anyone else. It's you."

My heart leapt at his words. The last time anyone had said "It's you" to me, they were blaming me for the relationship's demise. I turned, his arms still caged around me, and looked up into his eyes.

"There are things I want to tell you, things I'll need to tell you eventually, if we continue," I started, unsure of where the sudden bravery came from. "But until I can, until I feel like it's the right time or the right circumstance, I just need you to know that you make me happy."

His face changed from confused and worried to a smile so bright and joyful, I couldn't help but smile myself. And my God, he was handsome when he smiled. It never failed to make my breath catch. Before I could say anything ridiculous and embarrass myself, I stretched up and kissed him.

I kissed him softly, wanting to show him with the kiss that I was glad to be there, in his arms, at his house, with his kids. Happy to be with him. And I was. But what my kiss couldn't say were all the heavy thoughts and memories weighing down my heart.

My hands tentatively reached for his waist, gripping the shirt there, gently twisting the fabric in my fingers, wanting him closer. His fingers feathered over my cheeks as his hands came to cradle my face. His lips were soft against mine, answering my gentle kiss with a tender one of his own. He moved forward just a little, forcing me to step backward, my back pressing into the railing but my front pressing deliciously hard against his.

With every press of his lips against mine, every touch of his tongue against mine, the heaviness in my heart seemed to become lighter, or less noticeable. When he kissed me, I wasn't thinking about anything except his mouth on mine and his fingers threading through my hair. I was focused on how alive my body felt, how I was breathless for this man.

He eventually pulled away, like I knew he needed to, his forehead resting against mine as we both caught our breath.

"If my kids weren't in there…." He only sounded mildly irritated, but he laughed regardless.

"Your kids are great," I whispered, still trying to calm my body down from the effects of his kisses.

"Yeah." He sighed. Then his mouth pressed a kiss to my cheek and the rest of my defenses simply crumbled around us. "Shall we go see if Ruby's second batch of chocolate lava cakes turned out as good as the first?"

"You say chocolate and I'll follow you anywhere," I said with a smile, trying to hide the fact that I was falling desperately for the man right before his eyes.

He took my hand in his and led me inside, where the chocolate was just as good the second time around.

Chapter Fourteen

Grace

The door dinged as I pushed it open and I couldn't help but smile at how "small town" the hardware store seemed to be.

Devon was at the register and his eyes shot to me when he heard the bell. He gave me a sexy smile, but then went right back to ringing up the man who looked to be purchasing a medium-sized power tool. I would never be the woman who could name tools on sight, but the man buying it looked capable enough.

I slowly wandered through the back aisles of the store, not wanting to disrupt his work. As I strolled through, letting my eyes graze over the many different kinds of painting tape and drop cloths he carried, I listened as Devon exchanged remodel horror stories with the customer, laughing along with him when the man admitted to purposefully dropping a can of paint on the couch his wife loved but he loathed.

When the door finally dinged again, I heard Devon call out.

"I know you're back here somewhere." His voice was playful and coming from the middle of the store so I knew he'd moved away from the register. I turned in his direction. I smiled when he rounded the aisle I was in, his face splitting into that sexy grin at finding me. "Hey," he said as he closed the distance between us. "I wasn't expecting you."

"It's called a surprise," I said, holding up the brown paper sack that held my most favorite Chinese takeout. "I brought you lunch. Well, I brought us lunch. Do you have time?"

His hands slid around my waist as he said, "Time for takeout and my son's hot teacher? Yes. Yes, I have time."

I laughed as he kissed me. He took the bag from me, then took my hand and led me to the office that was located behind the register. He had a chair at his computer and a big comfortable recliner in the corner that I sat in immediately, loving the way is seemed to hug me.

"What brings you by?" he asked as he unloaded the iconic white boxes from the paper sack.

"Just thought it would be nice to bring you lunch," I said, shrugging. The truth of the matter was, my days and evenings had been filled with Devon and his family. Since the dinner at his house almost two weeks ago, we'd spent as much time together as possible. Most of that time involved Ruby and Jax, which I was thrilled about, but I knew his mother had them today while he worked, and it occurred to me we hadn't had much alone time since we really started seeing each other.

Sure, there were some evenings where the kids would go to bed and we'd find ourselves alone on his couch, but I was always nervous one of the kids would wander out looking for a drink of water or needing an extra check under the bed for monsters. Even though Devon tried relentlessly to act like teenagers by making out while watching a movie—which I didn't necessarily hate—I was always the one making sure we kept it family friendly.

Did I think much was going to happen in his office in the middle of the day at his hardware store? No. But it would still be nice to have a meal with him, just the two of us.

He filled my plate with my favorite foods, handed it to me, then dished up his own and took a seat behind his desk. I took a bite, sighing in delight, and my eyes rolled back in my head.

"There is nothing better than Chinese food," I mumbled around a full mouth.

"Second only to watching a beautiful woman enjoying it," Devon said with a wink.

"I have no shame when it comes to takeout. It's delicious. I don't care how bad it is for me."

"Grace, I just watched you wrap your lips around that fork and then moan. I'll buy you Chinese food every day for the rest of your life if that's the show you put on."

I blushed at his words but still couldn't find it in myself to be ashamed. So I shrugged and took another bite, loving the way my body reacted to the notion that he was aroused by me. He let out a rough laugh and then sat in his chair and propped his feet up on his desk, taking a bite of his fried rice.

We continued to eat, making small talk about our day. He told me a funny story about Jax and how he went to great lengths to annoy his sister that morning, and I told him about seeing a student in the grocery store with his mother who looked completely wrecked. A lot of the time students behaved much better for their teachers than their parents, so I knew that moms and dads were just as eager for school to start in the fall as teachers were for it to be over in the summer.

We were both laughing when we heard the door ding, but I was caught off guard to hear Devon's father call out from the back of the store, "I got it."

"I had no idea your dad was here," I whispered, mortified. "I would have brought him lunch, or at least made him a plate."

Devon set his lunch down and smiled. "Come here."

I looked out the window to make sure no customers nor his dad could see us, but then made my way over to him, putting my plate down on my chair. As I neared, his hands hit my hips and he positioned me against his desk, rolling his chair forward so that his knees straddled my legs. He looked up at me with lust in his eyes and his hands roamed from my hips down my legs, and up the backs of my thighs. For just a moment I regretted wearing jeans, wishing I'd put a skirt on to feel his fingers against my bare skin.

My breath picked up as his hands moved to cup my ass, pulling me away from the desk. Mine moved on their own and found purchase in his blond hair. I was practically in his lap and his face was mere inches from my sex, and even though I was fully dressed, it still felt dirty and illicit.

"Thank you for lunch," he said, his voice just a breathy growl. He pulled me even closer, his hands spanning the entirety of my ass. "I can think of a million ways to repay you. But all of them involve you out of these jeans and out of this office." His hands moved from my ass, forward, over my hips, his fingers spanning my body in the front, his thumbs dangerously close to the creases of my thighs. I was teetering between wanting his hands there so badly and wanting him to stop teasing me, to stop hinting at touching me in a way he couldn't possibly deliver on as we sat there in his office with his father just outside.

"Devon," I whispered, my fingers still threading through his hair, trying to imply with my tone that I wanted all those things done to me, but just not right that moment.

His fingertips dipped under the hem of my shirt and he slipped it up just barely, then leaned forward and pressed a kiss against my stomach, just below my belly button. His hands tightened on my waist, his mouth pressed against me harder, and he pulled me even closer to him, as if the space between us was offending him.

Two things happened next: my phone vibrated loudly from across the room and Devon's dad yelled for him from the back of the store.

"Devon, you know anything about this sand blaster?"

Devon's head fell softly forward, his forehead now resting against my belly. "Right now, I pretty much hate sand blasters," he said quietly, making me giggle. That only made his head bob against my belly, which made me giggle even more. When he pulled back he had a smile on his face too.

"You go help your father and I'll clean up lunch." I ran my fingers through his hair again, just because I wanted to, but then dropped my hands to my sides, not wanting to detain him any longer. He pushed his chair back, stood, dropped a quick kiss on my lips, and left the office with a smile.

"I'm not finished with you," he called as he walked through the doors, and I couldn't help but smile. There was a small garbage can beneath his desk, so I used it to collect the plates from our lunch, a stupid, lovesick smile on my face, and my phone buzzed again. I dug around in my purse, found my phone, and saw I had two messages from Shelby.

Hey lady, do you have a minute to talk?*

Give me a call as soon as you get a chance.

My best friend radar went on panic mode and I dialed her immediately. The phone only gave half a ring before she answered.

"Hey, Grace. How are you?"

"I'm fine, honey. How are you? What's wrong?" My mind started ticking off all the things she could be calling me about. Had something happened to her parents? Was she sick? Good God, what if it was cancer?

"I'm all right. I just wanted to talk to you about something. Do you have a minute?"

"Yeah," I said, confused. I sat back down in the recliner and could feel the tension building between my eyebrows, where my face was probably all tense and wrinkled.

"Are you sitting down?"

"Shelby, stop. You're worrying me. What's going on?"

"I ran into Jeff at the grocery store today."

There were many things in my life I'd changed in order to try and never hear that name again, or at least not for a long time. Hearing it caught me off guard and put my whole body on alert, but not the same way it would have three years ago, or even three months ago. I'd moved all the way to Florida to put as much space between my ex-husband and myself as possible, which made me wonder why Shelby thought she had to call me with a status update.

"Okay," I replied, drawing the word out, wondering where this conversation was going.

"He was with Jessica."

Now *that* name could always get a response from me. Hearing her name had a tendency to make me angry.

"And she was pregnant."

I went completely numb. The only sensation I could feel was my heartbeat pounding in my head, thumping wildly, deafeningly loud. Then my chest began to burn and I realized I was holding my breath.

"Grace? Are you there?" Shelby sounded tiny and very far away. "Grace, it's going to be all right." Her words cracked and somewhere in my mind I knew she was crying. Shelby had cried with me a lot over the years, but when Shelby cried, it was usually because she was worried about me. She'd seen me at my lowest point, the very bottom of a very black hole, and she'd watched me crumble. It was probably difficult for her to tell me this over the phone. She probably wanted to be right next to me when she said those words, to be able to look me in the eye and gauge whether or not I was about to spiral down the rabbit hole again. "Please, Grace, just say something."

"I'm here," I managed, although just those words were almost said in a sob. I needed to keep it together until I could be alone and have the breakdown I deserved.

"She looked miserable, sweetie. Real fat. Not just pregnant fat, but like she decided to eat for five, not two. And Jeff, he looked terrible too. Just awful. Eating for five as well."

I knew all of that wasn't true. Jessica probably looked great pregnant; even if she couldn't get rid of her resting bitch face or terrible personality, she wasn't bad looking. And it would take a lot to make Jeff unattractive. He had those all-American, boy-next-door looks.

"Shelby…." I wanted to tell her she didn't have to lie to me, didn't have to try and make me feel better.

"I wouldn't have even told you, but I know how word gets around, and I figured you'd rather hear it from me than someone else."

"Yeah." She was right about that. "I know."

"Oh, honey, I'm so sorry."

"It's okay, Shel. In the back of my mind I knew this would happen someday. Actually, I'm surprised it hasn't happened sooner." I tried to laugh, but I ended up crying a little, wiping a tear from under my eye before it could trail down my cheek.

"How can I help?" she asked, and she sounded genuine, as if she really needed to do something to help me.

"There's nothing to do. You've been there for me through everything. That's more than I can ask for." I heard heavy footsteps coming closer and panicked. "I've got to go, Shel. I'll call you later."

"Okay."

I hardly waited for her response before I ended the call, then turned my back to the door and wiped under my eyes again. Devon came in the room and the air changed instantly. Suddenly, everything was tense. He came toward me, his footsteps harder and surer than they were just moments before, and his hands gripped my shoulders. It wasn't painful, but it wasn't soft either.

"What is it?"

"No," I said quickly, trying to put on a brave face. "It's nothing."

"It's something, Grace."

I knew I had to look at him, to show him I was all right, to pretend as if everything was fine, if he was going to let me leave and have the breakdown I needed. So I lifted my face and put on a smile, weak as it may have been, and lied.

"Promise. Everything's fine. Shelby just called and was upset about something. But I do have to go," I said, breaking our gaze. I couldn't look him in the eye any longer. "Thank you for eating with me." I looked around, trying to seem too busy looking for my purse to pay him any attention, even though my whole body was tuned in to how tense he was, as if he were holding back and ready to snap at any moment.

We remained there for a few moments, me looking anywhere but at him, and him unmoving but breathing heavily. Finally, his hands took hold of my face with a strong but tender hold, and he dipped low to catch my gaze.

"I'll let you walk out of here, Grace. I'll let you leave and deal with whatever you have going on all alone, but I want to be very clear. I want to help you. I want to be with you. If you have a problem, I want to help you through it. But I do not want to chase after someone hoping to save them. Not again." He let out a sigh, but then took another sharp, deep breath and stepped closer. "Watching you walk away would hurt, but not as much as trailing after you."

The way his eyes bored into mine, the way his hands were holding on to me as if he didn't want to let me go, and his words, all came together and cut me open. A minute before I'd been prepared to walk out and spend an evening alone, crying in my apartment, but I didn't want to leave him behind. And more than that, I didn't want him to feel left behind either. It hadn't occurred to me that we'd both been left behind in the past. It hadn't occurred to him that we had that in common because, up until that moment, I'd avoided every opportunity to share with him why I'd gotten divorced and moved to Florida.

So, standing in the office of his hardware store with his hands framing my face and tears streaming down my cheeks, I brought Devon along with me.

"The only thing I wanted when Jeff and I got married was a family. We tried to get pregnant on our own, naturally, but it wasn't happening. When we sought help we were told there was something wrong with me, with my ovaries, and getting pregnant naturally was going to be an issue. I begged Jeff to try in vitro. I had to beg him because he didn't seem interested at all, which should have been my first warning sign, I'm sure. But I finally convinced him to let me try. It was weeks and weeks of hormone therapy coupled with two failed attempts. Two separate heartbreaking months of hoping and praying to be pregnant, only to have nothing show up on the scan. It was painful and emotionally destructive." I sucked in a breath and it came back out with a shudder. "And what I didn't know was that while I was sacrificing my body to make us a family, grieving every time it didn't work, Jeff was having an affair with his ex-girlfriend." My eyes closed, heavy with the weight of my words. Maybe it was because I was too tired to keep them open anymore, or perhaps I just didn't want to see Devon's face when he realized that I hadn't been woman enough to keep my husband.

"I couldn't give him a family, and for a while between rounds I couldn't give him my body. Apparently I wasn't enough. But now," I said, my voice catching on the sob lodged in my throat. "Now he's married to her and she's having his baby." The sob broke free and I collapsed against him, crying for so many reasons. Crying because my ex-husband cheated on me. Crying because I would never be the mother I so desperately longed to be. And crying because I had just told the man I'd hoped I could build some sort of life with exactly what kind of desolate future he would have if he stayed with me.

"Hey," he whispered into my hair between tender kisses against my temple. "Grace, don't cry, baby. Shhhh…." He held me as I sobbed, which both soothed and embarrassed me. "I know it sounds trite," he said as he slowly swayed me back and forth, trying to comfort me. "But any man who would cheat on you is an idiot." A tiny smile crossed my face, not that he could see it. "But any man who cheats on his wife while she's sacrificing herself to give him a child, well, he's an asshole." Devon pulled back and brushed all my crazy hair away from my face, looking me right in the eye. "And, baby, you deserve better than that."

He was right, but he was also wrong. Jeff had done something terrible to me, I could understand that. But there was always a bigger part of my brain that held on to the idea that he wouldn't have cheated on me if I'd been able to give him a child. When he'd married me, he expected a whole woman, but what he'd gotten was a broken one, a woman with something incredibly damaged inside her.

The most terrible part of my brain couldn't blame him for cheating.

"I'm sorry," I said, my voice hoarse from crying. "I should go."

"Grace, no," he said, his hands coming back to my shoulders. "Please stay and talk to me. If you leave now, I feel like you're just going to go home and have another breakdown."

I nodded, unable to vocalize that he was probably right.

"How can I make this better? What can I do?"

"It's not your job to make it better."

He pulled back at my words, like I'd insulted him, even though it was the last thing I wanted.

"I realize the man you were with treated you poorly. I'm sure I'll eventually hear more about the ways he treated the woman he was supposed to cherish, because there will be more with us, Grace. Not because it's my job, and not because I'm obligated, but because it's what I want. *You're* what I want." His hands slid down my arms and he laced his fingers through mine. "Nothing you just told me makes me want you less. It just makes me want to protect you more."

"I'm a mess," I cried. I wasn't sure if I was trying to push him away more or convince him, but he only laughed and pulled me closer.

"Remember the first time we met, Grace? I was a mess too. Something in the universe keeps pushing us together when we need it the most, and I don't know about you, but I'm done fighting the universe."

"It really is a stupid idea," I said, laughing and crying at the same time, but smiling too. Devon dipped again and kissed me softly.

"I'm sorry you went through all that," he said against my cheek as his mouth moved to my neck, pressing a kiss there, but then just resting, his arms wrapping around my waist. I curled my arms around his neck and let him hold me. "And I'm sorry the man who should have been there for you through the whole thing turned out to be a classic asshole." He sighed, his arms tightening around me. "But if I'm really honest, if he'd been a great guy, you wouldn't be in my arms right now."

Chills raced down my spine and goose bumps spread all over my arms. He was right. We'd both walked a terrible and sad road, but we'd found the way to each other. The past was in the past, and the future, in this moment perhaps, looked brighter because of the man in front of me.

"There's still a lot to talk about, but, for now, I'm glad we found each other. Again."

"Come talk to me over dinner at my house," he whispered, his face still buried in my neck.

"Okay," I replied, my voice a soft whisper. Because, honestly, how was I supposed to say no?

Chapter Fifteen

Devon

It had been an exhausting afternoon. After Grace left, I'd spent the rest of my day at work either worried about her, or really fucking pissed off at her ex-husband. What kind of douche bag lowlife cheats on his wife while she's trying to give him a child? For the rest of the day, anytime I helped a customer find a product, I only imagined all the ways I could use it to maim him. Rope? I'd tie that bastard up. Hand saw? That could do some damage. Ball peen hammer? Now we're talking.

My exhaustion must have showed on my face because as soon as I showed up at my parents' house to pick up the kids, my mom took one look at me, put her worried face on, and insisted on keeping the kids overnight. Ruby and Jax, who'd been camped in front of the television eating something that resembled every parent's worst sugar nightmare, didn't object. In fact, they didn't even look at me. They just waved over their heads and said they were fine sleeping over. So I left without them and realized I had an evening with Grace and no kids.

Suddenly, I wasn't so exhausted.

I sent her a text and let her know I'd be ready for her in an hour, then rushed home to shower and get dinner ready. I'd already razzled and dazzled her with my cooking skills, with Ruby's help, so I was going to rely on my grilling abilities. No one ever ate a good steak and regretted it. A perfectly cooked steak could be just as impressive as some other culinary masterpieces. That was what I was banking on, anyway.

When she knocked on my door, right on time, I opened it, grabbed her hand, pulled her in, and kissed her long and hard. She was giggling at first, laughing as though I was being playful. But after a few moments she realized I was not playing, and she melted against me.

She'd left her hair down and I wound my hands through it, pulling gently so her face angled up toward me. I walked her backward, using her body to close the front door, and pressed against her. Her hands were running up and down my back, pulling me closer, and I could feel every breath she took as her breasts pressed against my chest.

I could not get enough of her.

I'd been on board with taking our physical relationship slowly. There was a time and place for everything, and the time and place was not on my couch as my children slept down the hall. And as patient as I thought I was being, Grace had been *even more so*. Most of the time it had been her to stop us, to make us come up for air, before anything completely inappropriate took place. But in that moment, with her breathy whimpers and roaming hands, I wasn't sure we'd make it to the steaks.

"My mom is keeping the kids overnight," I said as I pressed kisses along the column of her neck, loving the way her body writhed against mine.

"Mmmm hmmm," she said, clearly unable to put words together, making me smile against her skin.

"Say you'll stay the night with me." She stilled at my words, and I was sort of expecting that. We'd had an emotional afternoon and she probably hadn't expected to be ambushed with sex when she agreed to dinner, but her hesitation was short-lived, and a moment later she was right back on track with me.

"Okay," she breathed.

"Here's what's going to happen," I said just before I took her earlobe between my teeth, tugging gently, then letting go. "I'm going to make us dinner, we're going to talk—about everything—and then we're going to bed." I pulled back and met her eyes. "Sound good?"

She nodded, her bottom lip trapped between her teeth.

"Good," I said, reaching up and gently tugging her lip free. "You're beautiful when you're frazzled." I tucked the hair I'd messed up behind her ear, smiling as I watched her senses come back.

"Frazzled," she said with a laugh. "That's a new word for it."

I kissed her then, because there was no way I couldn't. Then I took her hand and pulled her away from the door, leading her to the kitchen.

"Take these glasses of wine and go sit outside," I said, handing her the two glasses I'd poured just before she arrived. "I'll grab the food and meet you out there."

She complied, taking the wine outside, and my eyes stayed trained on her the whole time. I gathered everything I needed to cook our meal. We talked while I grilled, no residual awkwardness from that afternoon, our conversation flowing like it always had. When I watched her take the first bite of her steak, when her eyes rolled back in her head just like they had at lunch, I realized how much I loved that Grace enjoyed food. She wasn't shy about eating and something about that was sexy.

We talked about Jaxy and Ruby, about their upcoming trip to California, but neither of us admitted that we didn't miss them. Sure, a tiny part of me—the dad part—felt a little bit guilty that I was at home enjoying a real, adult meal, but the biggest part of me was glad my mom had offered to keep them. And I knew Grace was too.

When we were both done eating, I pushed my chair back and turned it, then crooked a finger at her.

"Come here, Grace."

She gave me a shy smile, but followed my instructions, walking around the table and stopping in front of me. I wrapped my arm around her waist and eased her down on my lap, pulling her close. She laughed and looped one arm around the back of my neck, giving me her signature bright smile.

"So," she said, laughing and swinging her legs. "Now's the part of the evening where we talk, huh?"

"Right," I said, settling my hand on her knee, making her legs still. "I want you to talk to me, but I want you to turn off your filter for a few minutes, and talk to me like you're not afraid of what the consequences might be."

"All right," she said, her voice unsure, her body tensing up.

"Hey." My hand on her knee moved to cup her face. "Don't do that, don't put up any walls. I just want to talk." She nodded, so I continued. "Tell me, honestly, the man you see yourself with for the rest of

Anie Michaels | 157

your life, how does he support you in regard to having children?"

Her eyes went wide with my question, but I simply slid my hand around the back of her neck and brought her forehead to mine. "It's okay, Grace. We're not making plans here, we're just talking. I want to know where your head is at, how you're feeling, and what you want in the future. Just talk to me." She nodded again, took in a deep breath, then relaxed a little as she exhaled. I loosened my hold on her, and we both leaned back. She bit her lip again, her eyes on the hand in her lap, fidgeting, but then eventually her gaze met mine.

"After everything that happened with Jeff, I'd pretty much resigned myself to never having kids. For a long time, I thought I'd never want to be with another man again. You know, scorned woman and all. I figured I'd be single forever and be a fabulous unmarried woman. But then the years passed and I realized I didn't want to be alone forever. The idea of dating again started to seep in, but I never did because every time I pictured myself dating a man, I pictured having the conversation with him I had with you today. And I always pictured him leaving afterward." She dropped her eyes again, looking down at her lap. "I mean, no man would want a barren woman."

"Hey, stop it," I whispered, squeezing her knee for emphasis.

She shrugged. "I'm being honest, Devon."

I couldn't argue with that. Honesty was what I'd asked for.

"Anyway," she continued. "If Jeff hadn't cheated on me, if we'd stayed together, I would have done another round of IVF. It was hard, and it was painful in all kinds of ways, but I would have done it again. So, I guess my future husband would have to be onboard for that. Or at least open to it." She shrugged again and let out a breath.

"What all does that entail?"

"It involves a lot. He would have to give me daily injections of hormones. It's a lot of doctor appointments, ejaculating into a cup, and watching me go through some painful procedures. It's crazy mood swings and a lot of emotional breakdowns." She sighed, pushing her brown locks out of her face. "It's also expensive, and not guaranteed. You end up spending twenty thousand dollars and in the end you might not even have a baby."

"I've spent twenty thousand dollars on things way less impressive than a baby," I said, trying to lighten the mood.

"Devon, don't," she chastised, her eyes darting downward again. "You wanted to have this conversation, and I knew it was coming, but don't joke around."

"Grace, look at me." She didn't, so I put a finger under her chin and brought her face up, looking her in the eyes. "I'm not joking, and I'm glad we're talking about this. Listen," I said, dropping my hand but shifting so both my hands were wrapped around her. "I'm not saying we're going to get married next week, but I wouldn't be with you if I didn't see a future. It wouldn't be fair to either of us, after what happened today, if we didn't talk about it. I don't want either of us to keep this up if it's just going to end down the line because we didn't talk about it."

"What are you saying?"

"I'm saying I want to know where your head's at, what you might want in the future."

"I want to be a mom."

"What about a stepmom?" With one question I'd moved us from the hypothetical to the reality. The switch was bold and the air changed around us. The conversation was suddenly very serious.

"I love Ruby and Jax, Devon. And if one day I got the chance to be their stepmother, I'd be honored. I'd love them and protect them, do anything I could for them. But...."

"But you'd still want a child of your own."

She nodded and I could see the tears welling in her eyes.

"Don't cry, Gracie. There's no reason to cry. If one day I get to be your husband, I'll do anything I can to make that happen for you."

"I would never want you or the kids to think you weren't enough for me, because I swear I would be happy with just us four, but if there's a chance—"

"I want to take that chance with you."

We stared at each other for a moment, our breaths panting in and out, both trying to take in the enormity of what we'd said to each other. I'd meant to have a conversation just to clear the air, to get everything out on the table, but I hadn't meant to talk seriously about marriage.

Not that I hadn't thought about it.

I had.

In passing.

I'd thought about marrying Grace when she helped Jaxy read a particularly hard word the week before last.

I'd thought about marrying Grace when she'd texted me to pick up some milk from the grocery store. I'd run out to rent a movie, and she and the kids decided to make cookies and didn't think there was enough milk for everyone.

I'd thought about marrying Grace when I watched her kiss Jaxy on the forehead as he lay asleep in his bed when she went in his room to tuck him in for the night.

I'd thought about marrying Grace when I discovered she hummed 80s music to herself when she does the dishes.

I'd thought about marrying Grace one night when we sat on the couch and she laughed at a stupid joke I'd made and pushed her hand through her hair at the same time.

I'd thought about marrying Grace that afternoon when she brought me lunch.

I'd thought about marrying Grace in that very moment, with her eyes staring back at mine, uncertainty clouding them, and I wanted nothing more than to reassure her I wasn't playing some hypothetical game. Grace, on paper, was perfect. But Grace, pulled apart, examined, identified, classified, quantified, and studied was whatever came after that. Something unnamed, because no one, aside from me, had taken the time with her. But I would.

My hand slid to the back of her neck, pulling her closer, and I kissed her. When she opened up for me, all the tension we'd built between us melted away. Our hands were both roaming wildly, her fingers threading through my hair, my hands gripping her waist, wanting nothing more than to feel her skin against mine.

Without much thought, I stood up, taking her with me, and carried her through the house all the way back to my bedroom, never taking my mouth away from hers. When I slowly laid her down on the bed, she seemed to blossom beneath me; arms above her head, legs open allowing me to rest between them, and eyes eagerly taking me in. She was just as engrossed in me as I was in her.

I wanted to tell her that I loved her, but I didn't want her to feel as though I was saying it for the wrong reasons. But, God, I loved her. I loved her in ways I'd thought might never be possible again. I felt things for her, cared for her in a way that I'd thought might have died. There'd been times in the past three years where I'd questioned my capacity for love, my capability, wondering if I'd ever love someone that deeply again, so I was grateful to have Grace in my arms, to be given the chance to love—and feel loved—again.

She hadn't said it, and neither had I, but I felt what I thought was love coming from her. I felt it in the way she kissed me, in the way her hands skimmed up my back, and in the way she looked at me with trust emblazoned in her eyes.

"I'd never do anything to hurt you." My words were whispered against the skin of her neck as my hands skimmed up her torso under her shirt. She gasped, her back bending, bringing her chest closer. My thumbs brushed the skin just below her breasts and I felt her shudder. "It's been a long time for me, Grace. I'm going to need you to say something. Let me know you're all right."

"I want this," she said, arching her back further. "I want you, Devon." Her hands smoothed up my arms and over my shoulders, pulling at my shirt. I leaned back to pull it off and watched as she slid her shirt up and over her head as well.

My mouth immediately went to the swell of her breast, my hand cupping the other over her bra. Slowly, pieces of clothing came off and we explored each other's bodies. We were in no hurry and I took every opportunity to memorize and taste every part of her.

We were hot breaths, writhing bodies, and thumping heartbeats.

"Devon," she rasped, slowly coming down from a high. "I don't want anything between us."

I stilled at her words, caught off guard. There were condoms just a few feet from us in my nightstand. I'd made a special trip to the drug store on my own to make the purchase, but hearing those words from her caused all the breath to leave my lungs. The idea that she would give me her body, trust me in that way, and leave nothing between us, it cracked something inside me open.

"Grace," I said, just before kissing her, "are you sure?"

"I'm clean," she said urgently. "Every test I've had since my marriage ended has been clear." She bit her lip and brought her hand to my cheek. "I've never felt so connected to someone, and I don't want anything between us. Ever."

"I've only been with one person that way."

"I trust you," she said as her thumb stroked my cheek.

"I trust you too." My body was at its breaking point and wanted to find that high with her. "I want it too, Grace. I want to feel all of you, more than anything, but you have to know I didn't anticipate this. I wasn't expecting it at all."

"I know. I wasn't either. But being with you, here, in your arms, with your skin against mine, putting a barrier between us would feel wrong. And I want to feel everything." She said the words as her body moved closer, tilting toward me.

I couldn't hold back any longer. I leaned back down, kissing her as I entered her, both of us groaning at the connection.

The next few hours were spent in each other's arms, finding every way we could to make each other's bodies sing. So many times I wanted to tell her how I felt, that I loved her, that I needed more than just her body, but her heart and her soul as well. I thought perhaps I saw the same war going on inside her eyes, so I spent the time, instead, using my body to say the words.

Chapter Sixteen

Devon

Grace had been spending nights at my house for a while, but she had a tendency to not want the kids to see her there in the mornings. I understood, but I didn't necessarily agree. I wanted the kids to get used to her being around, at any time of day. But I also didn't want to make Grace uncomfortable. That was why I stood against the doorjamb and watched her car pull away from the curb, giving her a wave.

She was fucking beautiful in the mornings and it was difficult to let her out of bed.

We spent long nights making love, then she'd disappear as soon as the sun came up, and each time I wanted to hold her to me, to make her stay.

Once her car was out of sight I shut the door and moved toward the kitchen to put my coffee cup in the sink.

My eyes were caught by the picture of Olivia hanging in the living room.

When we'd first moved to Florida, I was still trying to process Olivia's death and even though I knew being close to my parents would help all of us, I didn't want my kids to leave Olivia behind. I was afraid that moving from the home they'd had with her to a new one with no part of her would be upsetting. So I made sure Olivia was there, as much as she could be.

My eyes wandered throughout the living room and I took in all the photos of her. Every photo was intentional. I'd put them there so Ruby and Jax could see her and even, perhaps, feel her there. And in the beginning, it worked. I saw her face all the time.

But now, the photos were fading into the background. I only saw them if I looked for them. And I hadn't been looking very often.

I put my coffee cup in the sink and decided to make the kids a big breakfast, or as big as I could manage. Pancakes and eggs were about my limit. One day I needed to figure out how to cook bacon on the grill outside. My mind was working on the difficult thoughts, milling them around, breaking them down, as I put the pancake mix, eggs, and milk together in the bowl and started mixing.

I made twenty pancakes and scrambled and cooked eight eggs, and my mind still hadn't worked everything out.

When the sounds of children waking and moving around started to filter in from down the hall, I knew it would only be a few minutes before Ruby and Jaxy made their way to the kitchen, led by their noses. Going all out, I set the table, ready to have a family breakfast.

"Daddy," Jaxy cried excitedly. "Did you make pancakes for breakfast?"

"Sure did, bud." I pulled his chair out for him and he practically dove for it, eyes trained on the giant stack of pancakes before him. "Eggs, too."

"Best dad ever!"

"Is it somebody's birthday?" Ruby asked, coming into the kitchen from the hallway, eyes on the food as well.

"Nope. I was just up early and thought you guys could use a good breakfast."

Ruby shrugged and took her seat.

We all filled our plates with food and dug in, the kids talking with full mouths, telling me what their plans were for the weekend. Most of the plans included video games and playing with the kids who lived down the street. Normal kid stuff. And it hurt my heart, but I had to bring up the topic that no kid should have to deal with.

Placing my fork down, I laced my fingers together and pressed them against my lips, trying to find the right words.

"Ruby, Jax, I have a question," I started, my voice wavering just the slightest. I was nervous, but I didn't want them to see that. "How would you guys feel about redecorating the living room?"

Ruby's eyes wandered to the room in question, and Jaxy simply shrugged, said, "Okay," and then crammed another forkful of pancake into his mouth.

"You mean, like, new paint and throw pillows?" Ruby asked, a little more suspicious than her brother.

"We could paint," I said, nodding, still struggling. "How would you guys feel if we took down some of the photos of your mom?" Both kids stilled and the room was silent. My breath stalled and my throat was dry.

"Why do we have to take them down?" This came from Jaxy. He looked more confused than hurt, so

I was glad about that. I could deal with confusion, but I didn't want to hurt my kids.

"We don't have to take them down, bud. I was just looking at the living room this morning and noticed there are a lot of pictures of her. And that's great. We can leave them up if you want, but I just thought maybe it was time to take some down."

He turned his head and looked in the living room for a moment, then turned back to me, expressionless. I had no idea what was going on in his head.

"But then she'll be gone." This came from Ruby, and it was everything I'd hoped to avoid.

"Sweetie, she'll never be gone, not all the way. We still think about her and remember her, and celebrate her birthday, and we always will. And if you guys really want the pictures to stay up, we can leave them. It was just a thought."

"Do you think they bother Grace?"

Ruby voiced the very thought that prompted the whole discussion. The last thing I wanted was the kids to think Grace had anything to do with it. I in no way wanted them to associate the two ideas. So I shook my head.

"No. I don't think it bothers her at all."

That was the truth.

But it bothered *me*.

I loved Olivia and had she lived I was sure we would still be married and happy. But she didn't. And the strangest part about being a widower was moving on and dating someone else when I never really fell out of love with my wife. In the beginning it felt a little bit wrong. But the thing about grieving is everything feels wrong, until it doesn't. The only way to get past it is to keep moving forward.

I was sure Grace would never ask me to take down photos of Olivia, but that's one of the things I loved about her. I wouldn't want to be with someone who would storm in and expect my kids and me to erase Olivia from our lives. Besides being unreasonable, it was impossible. But even though Grace would never ask it of me, it didn't mean it shouldn't happen.

"Listen, guys, there are plenty of ways to keep your mother around. We can talk about her, talk about our memories, tell Grace all about her. I know Grace would love to hear about your mother and how wonderful she was." The best part about that statement was that I knew it was true. Grace would feel honored if the children shared their stories of Olivia with her. "What if you each choose a photo from the living room and you can keep it in your bedroom. That way, we aren't taking them down, but just moving them."

"We can pick any one we want?" Jaxy asked, perking up.

"Yeah, bud. Any one you want."

He got up from his chair and ran into the living room. "I want the one where I'm just a baby and Mom is looking at me and she's all sweaty." He stepped up on to the edge of the fireplace and grabbed the photo off the mantel. "This one's my favorite because Mommy always said it was the moment she fell in love with me."

He didn't even have to show me the photo for me to know which one he was talking about. I'd taken the photo about two minutes after he'd been born and Olivia had refused to hand him over to the nurses. She just kept touching his chubby cheeks and saying, "He's so beautiful," over and over again. When the nurses finally convinced her to let them measure and weigh him, she'd just stared at him from across the room.

I shook the memory away, trying not to get too caught up in the past. My kids needed me present in that moment. Jaxy ran down the hall with his photo and I assumed he was going to find the perfect spot for it in his room.

"Ruby, is this plan all right with you?" She was nibbling on her lower lip. "Come here," I said, crooking a finger at her. She stood up slowly and made her way toward me. When she was close enough, I grabbed her and hauled her into my lap, pulling her shoulder into my chest and wrapping both my arms around her. "Talk to me, Rubster."

She took in a deep breath, her shoulders tightening, but then she exhaled, all the tension leaving with her breath. "I used to sit on the couch, when we first moved here, and just look at all the pictures of Mommy. In the beginning, it kind of made me sad, you know? But then, after a while, I liked seeing her there and remembering all the times we took the photos. But now that we're talking about taking them down, I just…."

"It's okay, Ruby. Whatever you're feeling is totally okay. And whatever you're afraid to say, you don't have to be. You can't say anything wrong in this situation."

Her eyes lifted to meet mine and I gave her a squeeze, and then, finally, she spoke.

"I just realized, now that we're talking about taking them down, I don't even really look at them anymore." I heard sadness in her voice and guilt. I knew that guilt. Sometimes, surviving came with the heaviest guilt and it came out of nowhere. You were just living your life, trying to move on, and suddenly you realized your wife would no longer be able to sit in the school pickup line and you crumble under a wave of guilt. Survivor's guilt. I hated it, but I also knew it was part of grieving.

"You might not remember this, baby, but one of the things your mom was very adamant about was that you and your brother needed to be kids. She didn't want you worrying about this kind of stuff. She wants you to be eleven and play outside with your friends. She wants you to stay up too late reading and not let boys pick on you in school. She doesn't want you sitting in the living room staring at her photos. She wants you to be a kid and to be happy and playful and funny." I felt Ruby turn her face in to my chest and I knew she was getting upset. "Baby, it's okay to be sad sometimes, and to miss her, but you don't have to feel bad for not missing her enough. There's no such thing. However you feel, however often you think about her, that's the exact right amount, sweetie."

"I just don't want her to think I don't love her anymore." She said the words on a sob and pressed her face even farther into me.

That was the part that sucked the most. I was constantly torn between wishing my kids didn't have to deal with this grief, and being grateful they'd had Olivia for even a few years. It was a constant emotional battle and some days were harder than others.

"Your mother knows exactly how much you love her, Ruby. And photos in the living room don't make you love her more or less, right? It doesn't matter what's on the mantle, it's what's in here." I pressed my hand to her chest, still hugging her to me. "You carry her with you in here."

I held her for a few minutes more while she cried quietly, grateful Jaxy had found something to occupy himself for a few moments. When she finally settled and pulled back, I tipped her face up to look at me, my hands around her still round, but thinning out, face.

"We don't have to take them down if you don't want to."

"No," she said, wiping her eyes. "It's okay. But maybe…."

"What, baby?"

"Can we just leave one out? Just so that she isn't gone completely."

"Of course," I said as I pressed a kiss against her forehead.

Ruby hopped off my lap and walked to the mantle, her eyes scanning over the photos. She grabbed a frame, held it to her chest, and walked back to her bedroom.

I didn't have to see the photo to know which one it was. It was Ruby's fifth birthday party, right before Olivia's diagnosis. Olivia had just sung happy birthday and placed a big cake with five candles in front of Ruby. Everyone in the photo was looking at Ruby, including Olivia, but Ruby was looking up at her mother, smiling and laughing. It was one of the last moments we had as a family before everything changed. It was, quite possibly, the last untainted moment captured between the two of them.

That night while the kids slept, I packed the rest of the photos into boxes. I pulled down the huge print of Olivia on our wedding day that hung in the place of honor, wrapped it in newspaper, and stored it in the garage. I left the throw blanket Olivia had crocheted while pregnant with Jaxy on the couch, and one photo on the mantle of the four of us. Olivia would never fully be gone, and I didn't want her to be. She would always be a part of our lives, even if it was always in the past. I didn't want my kids to think I was throwing her away, or trying to erase her, so I left one photo up to remind us all of what we lost, but also to remind us to live a great life because Olivia couldn't.

When I went to bed that evening, I took the wedding photo that I'd placed on my dresser when I moved in, wrapped it in one of Olivia's scarves, and put it in the back of the closet.

A few nights later, the kids were in bed and Grace was on the couch with me. We'd had dinner then played a game of UNO with the kids that seemed to last forever, but once they were in bed, the house was quiet, and so was Grace. I was half sitting and half lying, my back propped up against the arm of the couch, legs sprawled out wide with one foot on the floor. Grace was lying on her chest, cheek resting against her hands, which were laced together and resting on my chest. My fingers were trailing mindlessly through her hair, gliding through without any effort, the motion soothing. Something was on the television, something she'd settled on, but I wasn't paying attention and I wasn't really sure she was either. Her breaths were even, her body relaxed.

Twenty minutes had passed and not a word was spoken.

When Grace lifted her head and met my eyes, hers were full of thought and worry.

"All the photos of Olivia are gone." It wasn't a question, but she was wondering about it. Perhaps she didn't know what she was asking, or if she even had the right to ask.

"Not all of them," I said, pushing her hair over her shoulder, allowing me to see her whole face. "The kids each picked one to keep in their room, and I left one up of all four of us. But the rest are put away. It was time." My thumb stroked her cheek, watching as her eyes gave away all the thinking going on in her head. I brought my thumb down her face, over her chin, then up a little to feather over her bottom lip, trying to keep it from hiding between her teeth.

"I never would have—"

"I know. And that's one of the things I love about you."

She stilled at my words, but spoke almost immediately.

"There's more than one?"

"There's a lot. I find a new reason every day. Sometimes two."

"Devon," she whispered. I could tell my words were scaring her, but I hoped it was scaring her because she felt the same way, and not because she didn't. So I did stop, but only because I grabbed her under her arms and pulled her up my body, bringing her mouth right to mine.

A whisper-quiet moan escaped her, but then her mouth answered mine, parting her lips and welcoming me in. My hands roamed her back, tangled in her hair, and held her close to me. Her hands found the sides of my neck and held on, her hair falling like a veil around us.

She let me kiss her, if only for a few moments, before she pulled away with a worried look on her face.

"Devon, please, we have to talk about this."

"About what?" I asked, still playing with the hair that was draped around us. "The pictures, or me loving you?"

"Both," she said, the word falling from her mouth on a breath.

I kissed her again, this time wrapping my arms around her and rolling her under me. I wanted her totally present for the conversation and didn't want her wiggling away from me—either emotionally or physically. We were going to talk about this until it was clear to her that she was it for me.

She let out a tiny squeal when she realized what I was doing, and I pushed up on one arm so as not to squish her beneath me. My other arm was next to her head, my hand still in her hair.

"It was time for the pictures to go, Grace. Regardless of my dating status, we don't need a shrine to Olivia in the living room. There are still plenty of photos around the house and in the kids' bedrooms, and I can always pull them out of the garage when the kids want to look at them. I didn't take them down for your sake. But I'm not going to lie and say you, and my feelings for you, didn't have something to do with it."

"You'd be doing it even if I wasn't in the picture?"

"Eventually." I could tell my answer made her uncomfortable, so I simply leaned down and kissed her. I nipped at her bottom lip until she opened for me, and then swept my tongue through her mouth, trying to convey even one fraction of the way I felt about her in our kiss. It was deep, passionate, all-consuming, and made me breathless. "I don't want to talk about the pictures anymore," I said, pulling back slightly. Only enough so that I could speak.

"Okay," she whispered back. "What should we talk about?"

I kissed her bottom lip again, this time tugging gently on it only because I knew she liked it. I was

174 | The Presence of Grace

rewarded with a small groan from her. I smiled, moving my lips over her cheek and down her throat. "I want to talk about how much I love you," I said against her neck, grinning when she moved her head to the side, giving me better access.

"How much?" she said, half moaning the words and half pushing them out on a breath.

"More than is reasonable," I said, smiling against her. I placed one more kiss against her neck, just behind her ear where I knew she liked it, then pulled up to look her in the eye. "I love you, Grace. More than I think I deserve to, sometimes. I don't know how I got so lucky to find you, to find this happiness again, but I'll never stop trying to make you feel my love for you."

Her hand ran up my chest, stopping right over my heart where I was sure she could feel it thumping. "I love you too. I love you. And I'm so scared," she whispered, her eyes narrowing.

"I know," I said, my voice matching hers. "But I promise you've got nothing to be afraid of. I'll spend the rest of my life loving you, if you'll let me."

"I want that."

I leaned down and kissed her again, slowly this time, letting our words seep into her, hoping they'd fill some of the cracks I knew were left behind.

"Do you remember the first night we met?" I whispered to her a while later as we lay in my bed, nothing between us except love.

"Back in Fairbanks?" she asked, drawing a circle on my chest with just her finger.

"Yeah."

"Of course." She looked up at me, gorgeous hair crazy and wild, eyes so blue that not even the ocean could compare.

"I remember telling you that every day I woke up and only hoped that day would be better than the last."

"I remember that too."

"You make every day better, Grace."

Chapter Seventeen

Grace

"Oh, God, that's good." My eyes closed and my head dropped back as I savored the first sip of coffee that morning. Devon hadn't let me sleep at my apartment in days, and I was still paranoid about the kids finding me there, so I'd been getting up at the crack of dawn and it was beginning to take its toll.

Curling up in my recliner next to the window in my living room, I let my thoughts drift back to the night before and all the revelations Devon had shared with me. With my coffee cup resting on my knee, my hands still wrapped around it for its warmth, I let my head fall to the side, against the smooth leather of the chair. My eyes closed and immediately the images of Devon from the night before flooded my mind.

His face as he told me he loved me. The way his eyes stared right into mine as he moved over me, inside of me. The sincerity in his eyes as he spoke of our future together and what he saw for us.

The sound of my phone vibrating against the wood of my end table snapped my eyes open, and I saw Shelby was trying to FaceTime me. I accepted the call and then smiled when her face appeared on my screen.

"Hey, you," I said.

"Oh, look, you're alive and answering your phone. And at your own house, believe it or not." Her tone was playful and teasing, but I still blushed, a little embarrassed to be one of those people who disappeared at the beginning of a new relationship.

"I'm sorry."

"Are you kidding? Do not even think of apologizing. You can make everything up to me by telling me, in explicit detail, everything that's been happening while you haven't been returning my calls." Shelby sat down on her own couch, pulled her fuzzy blanket she'd had since college over her legs, and got comfortable with her own cup of coffee. "Spill," she demanded.

"I don't really know what to say." I laughed, blushing even harder.

"Did you sleep with him?"

My mouth dropped open in surprise at her forward question, but then I snapped it closed when I remembered that Shelby was anything but subtle.

"That's pretty personal," I said, trying to keep the answer from being evident on my face.

"So, that's a yes." She let out a happy squeal and I could see her bouncing up and down on her couch. "Was it amazing? Mind-blowing? Did you have an out-of-body experience?"

All I could do was blink in response.

"Oh, no. Was it terrible?" she asked, concern written all over her face.

"No," I exclaimed loudly. "It wasn't terrible at all. It was… wonderful." The blush crept back over my face so I hid it in my arm, the warmth burning in my cheeks.

"Oh, Gracie, I'm so happy for you." Shelby's voice was softer and I looked up. "Now, tell me all about it."

I laughed and took another sip of my coffee, letting her squirm in her seat. "Shel, you know I don't kiss and tell."

"Okay, fine. You can skip all the sexy details, but I wanna know how everything is going. Talk to me.

I have to live vicariously through you! I'm wilting away here in Fairbanks all alone. Every single man over twenty-five is either still living with his parents or a complete douche nozzle. So, tell me about Devon and how wonderful he is."

"It's hard to explain," I started, unable to find the exact words. "He's patient and caring, and a wonderful father, and God, so sexy." I think for a moment, trying to get the words straight in my mind. "Before I ran into Devon a few months ago, I thought I had my shit together, you know? I was moving on, had my dream job, was making a life for myself here. But then Devon shows up and all of sudden I've got more insecurities than I know what to do with, and I feel like a crazy person."

"What do you mean?"

"Devon's a single father and a widower."

"Right. And?"

"So, logically, he should be the insecure one in the relationship, right? He should need the time and the coddling and the reassurance. He should need things to go slow. But it's like all the roles are reversed and even though I thought I had my shit together, being with him—even though it's wonderful—is making me go a little crazy."

"How so?"

"Last night when I got to his house, he'd taken down most of the photos of his wife. And there had been quite a few. It was pretty noticeable they were missing."

"Okay...."

"So I kind of flipped out on the inside."

"Why?" Shelby asked, laughing.

"Because I don't want him to think that I want to take her place! I don't want his kids to think I want to take her place either!"

"So you would have liked him to leave the photos up forever?"

"No, I just wish it didn't have anything to do with me."

"Maybe it doesn't."

"Listen, my situation with Jeff was very different from Devon's with his wife. I know, without a doubt, I'm done with Jeff. I want nothing to do with him, at all. And even though this makes me a *terrible* person, it's hard to think about the idea that Devon would choose to be with Olivia over me."

"Oh, sweetie," Shelby started, and I knew she was going to say something nice and supportive, and I didn't want to hear it.

"I feel like shit for even thinking these thoughts, but I can't help it. How do you know, when your wife dies, that it's time to move on? How can he be so serious about me so quickly, when he hasn't been with anyone since? What if he realizes he's made a mistake and he's not over her? I'm just supposed to hope for the best? I've put my heart on the line like that before and it didn't end well. Not for me, anyhow."

"Grace," Shelby whispered, trying to keep me from plummeting into the dark, emotional abyss I was currently circling. "Things with Devon have got to be complicated—dating a man with children always is— but you have to either trust him, or let him go, honey." The idea of letting him go made my stomach roll and turn over. "I can't imagine what it would be like."

"How can he be in love with his wife one day, watch her *die*, and then fall in love again? I mean, I know in theory it happens, but I never thought I would be in this situation. How does someone ever really get over the death of their spouse?" I was asking the universe because I knew Shelby didn't have the answer. Neither of us did. Devon probably didn't either. Which was almost what made the whole thing so damn frustrating. I would never know, for sure, where I stood in comparison. Was he with me only because she was gone? If she were still alive, would they be together? And if so, what if we'd met then? Would he have left her for me? What if he and I were together first and then he met her? There were so many unanswerable questions, so many variables that I would absolutely never get a firm consensus on because Olivia had died. I let out a hard breath, then shook my head. "Man, I am such a bitch."

"You're not. This is a hard situation and you're just being honest. That's what best friends are for. You get to say all the wrong things to me so you don't say them to Devon and screw everything up. You don't want to screw everything up, do you?" Her question was serious and I knew she wanted an honest answer.

"No, I don't want to screw everything up. But I also don't want to be emotionally torn to shreds in a few weeks when he realizes he's still in love with his wife. Ex-wife. Dead wife. Shit." I pulled my knees up to my chest, placing my coffee cup on the table.

"Listen, from everything I've ever heard about Devon, and from the few times I spent any significant time with him, I can tell you I think he's a really decent guy. Like, a really *good* guy, Grace. And I don't think he's going to break your heart. I do think it's really important that you talk to him about this. Only he can tell you exactly what he's thinking or how he's feeling."

My mind drifts back to our conversation the night before on his couch and I shut my eyes, groaning. I didn't really want to have that conversation again, but I knew she was right. I had to tell him why I was pulling away. If I didn't, eventually I would pull right out of his grasp and he'd have no option but to let me go.

"Don't sabotage a good thing because your ex-husband did a number on you. Don't let Jeff and that Jessica bitch have that much power over you."

I had to laugh at Shelby's obligatory best-friend-mistress-hating skills.

"You're right. I know you're right. But…."

"What? Spit it out."

"What if I say all this to him and he thinks I'm a terrible person. I *feel* like a terrible person."

"Grace, Devon loves you. He probably realizes there's something wrong and is waiting for you to be comfortable enough to tell him what it is. Put the man out of his misery. The sooner you tell him what's bothering you, the sooner he can make you feel better with his penis."

"Shelby!" I couldn't help the laughter that escaped me, and eventually there were tears streaming down my face. "You're the only person in the world who could say something like that to me and make me laugh. Those words from anyone else would just be wrong."

"Hey, it's my job to make you laugh. It's also my job to tell you when you're being dumb. You're not being dumb yet, but if you don't tell him about all this, you'll be on your way there."

"I know."

"When do you see him next?"

"I'm supposed to go over there after my shift tonight."

"I expect a full report tomorrow. And not just a report about the conversation, although that's important. I put in my best friend time today, doled out my best advice, and I require compensation in the form of sexy details."

"Sexy details? What kind of details are you looking for?"

"General girl talk. Length. Girth. Stamina."

"I'm not talking to you about his *girth*." I couldn't even say the word without blushing.

"Fine. Be that way."

I sighed, then smiled.

"Thanks for being an awesome friend, Shel."

"Takes one to know one," she said, winking, making me smile even wider.

Work was uneventful, but for the first time all summer I found myself irritated with the bar scene. The tips were good and it helped bridge the gap between the end of one school year and the beginning of another, but there were only so many ways you could tell drunken twentysomethings that you weren't interested in going home with them. Also, the guys who ordered drinks with sexual titles always seemed to think that if you heard them say those words, you would magically fall into bed with them. If I never heard another man order a Sex on the Beach or a Buttery Nipple, it would be too soon.

Halfway through my shift, the bar was packed. The music was loud and the people were rude, and even though it was no different than any other night, it all just rubbed me the wrong way. Next summer I needed to consider finding something different.

A loud crash at the front door caught my attention and I turned to see what was happening, but all I saw was Randy wrestling someone out the door. I shook my head. Randy didn't have to throw someone out every night, but it happened more often than I'd imagined it would. A woman at the end of my bar caught my attention when she waved at me, signaling she wanted to order a drink. I wiped the bar on my way down to her, and then got back to work.

An hour later, Randy appeared at my bar.

"Hey, Grace. Time for break."

"Okay," I said, my head tilting with my confusion. Randy was never the one to send me to break.

"Let me walk you back to the break room."

Nodding, I followed him down the darkened hallway. When we stepped into the small break room he turned around to face me.

"Earlier I had to throw a guy out of the bar."

"Yeah, I saw that. Was he causing problems?"

"It was the guy who attacked you out back a few weeks ago."

His words made all the hair on my arms stand up and my heart plummet to the bottom of my lungs.

"What?"

"Yeah. I saw him a few seconds after he got in, and I grabbed him like *that*." He said the words with a snap of his fingers. "I don't care if you pressed charges or not, he's not allowed in this bar. But I wanted to let you know he came back. I can't be sure he would have bothered you, but I wasn't willing to take the chance."

"Thanks, Randy. I appreciate it." My stomach was rolling and I was suddenly queasy.

"Did you end up filing a restraining order?"

I shook my head. "I guess I figured I didn't need to."

"Maybe it wouldn't be such a bad idea."

"Yeah. I think you might be right."

"You okay to stay and finish your shift? You can leave if you need to."

"No, I'm all right. I just need a few minutes."

Randy nodded. "You let me know if you need anything, and I'm walking you out to your car tonight after shift."

"You always walk me to my car after shift."

"Damn straight," he said, giving me a friendly wink.

"Thank you."

"Anytime, darlin'."

By the time my shift was over, I was exhausted and just wanted to curl up and go to sleep. But I knew I wanted to curl up and fall asleep with Devon's arms around me, so I mustered up the courage to drive to his house, even though I knew we'd have to talk about everything roaming around in my head.

As usual, Devon's door was unlocked so I let myself in quietly, locking it behind me. He always left the light over the stove on for me, but it was still a dark walk back to his bedroom. On the way, I peeked into Jax's room, noting the nightlight was still on, which was good because if he woke up in the middle of the night and it was off, he'd panic. When I passed Ruby's door I opened it just a crack and watched her for a moment, looking for the silent rise and fall of her chest.

Convinced both the kids were good for the night, I made my way to the end of the hall where Devon's door was. When I pushed it open a wave of humidity rolled over me and I saw him sitting on the edge of his bed.

"Kids good?" he asked with a smile.

"Yeah." I returned his smile then placed my purse on the chair by the window. "Why is it so steamy in here?"

"I drew you a bath."

"You drew me a bath?" I asked, laughing at his choice of words.

"Yeah. It won't sound so funny when you're soaking in the hot water with a glass of wine."

"You're right. That doesn't sound funny. It sounds wonderful." I stepped up to him and smiled as his hands seemed to naturally move to the backs of my thighs, pulling me closer. "Are there bubbles?"

"Do you need bubbles?" His hands ran up my legs, fingers sliding under the edge of my skirt, flirting with the lace of my panties.

"Hmmm. Maybe not, but only if you join me." His hands fell from my legs, which I was upset about at first, but he stood, pulling his shirt over his head, and I was too caught up in watching him undress to worry about much else.

We both took our clothes off, eyeing the other, then he led me to the bathroom where the deep, jetted tub was full, steam still coming off the water. And sure enough, in the back corner sat a glass of white wine, condensation forming on the outside of the glass.

Silently, he stepped into the tub, scooting his body back, leaving enough room for me to climb in front of him. Once we were both settled, my back against his front, one of his arms wrapped around the front of my shoulders, his other hand holding mine, only then could I feel myself start to really relax. A few quiet moments passed. I used my free hand to push the hot water up to my neck, loving the feeling of the water lapping against me.

"Tell me what's bothering you," he whispered against my ear.

Taking a deep breath, I prepared to say the words I knew would upset him. "The guy who attacked me at the bar showed up again tonight." I felt him tense beneath me. His whole body contracted, hard like stone. "Randy spotted him before he really got in and kicked him out, but I can't understand why he'd come back."

"We're going to the police station and filing a restraining order tomorrow." I nodded, in complete agreement. "And you're not working at a bar next summer. I don't care what it takes, you're not walking into a place where drunken idiots can get their hands on you all night."

I ran my hand up his arm, trying to calm him. I was upset at first when Randy first told me what had happened, but I'd had a few hours to calm down. Devon was in the middle of the adrenaline rush, at the apex of the rage. I knew he wasn't angry at me, but at the situation, and I just wanted to soothe him.

"I was thinking about that earlier today, even before he showed up. There are other ways I can make money in the summertime. I can tutor or even just get a normal waitressing job in a nice restaurant. No more bars. I only have two weeks left anyway. Summer's almost over."

"No more bars," he practically growled. The words sounded more possessive than predatory, and even though it was slightly inappropriate considering the circumstances, I couldn't help the fact that his voice did things to my body. "Tomorrow we go to the police station. My mom can watch the kids."

"Okay," I said, my voice breathy and soft.

He was quiet for a few minutes and as they ticked by his body slowly relaxed beneath me. I kept running my hand over his arm, splashing warm water on our bodies, just enjoying the way it felt to be held by him.

"You've been off for a few days, Grace. This isn't just about what happened tonight. I can feel it. I know something else is bothering you. I just wish you'd tell me." He paused for a moment, then gave my hand a squeeze before he spoke again. "Are you still worried about the photos?"

I tried not to react to his words. His breath against my skin made goose bumps break out, but the reason behind his words made me tense as I remembered the conversation I'd had with Shelby and all the things I still had to tell him. "I don't know. Sort of. I think the photos just made me start thinking, and that was a bad idea in general."

"What do you mean?"

"Before I unload on you, I just kind of want some sort of reassurance that you won't think less of me afterward. I feel like a shitty person already, so just promise me you won't hold it against me."

"Babe, as long as what you're saying is how you really feel, I'll never think less of you. I might not always agree, but I'll never look down on you for how you feel about something." After he said the words, he pressed his lips against my neck and I cherished the connection, fearing it would be gone soon and I'd never have it again.

I took a deep breath and hoped this wasn't the last conversation we'd have as a couple. I knew I had to talk to him about it, to let him either make me feel better or confirm my fears. Either way, it wasn't fair to him to keep the thoughts to myself any longer. "You know you don't have to worry about Jeff, right?"

"What do you mean?" Confusion laced his voice.

"I mean, if Jeff showed up on my doorstep next week, I'd tell him to go to hell. I'd slam the door in his face. He'd have no shot. You believe me, right?"

"Yeah," he replied, still confused.

"Why do you believe me?" I asked, hoping to prove a point.

He didn't answer right away, but eventually said, "Because you're with me now." My lungs snagged on a breath.

Damn.

When I didn't respond immediately, his arm around my shoulders squeezed. "Talk to me."

"You didn't have a nasty divorce from your wife. You didn't have a falling out, or even a fight. When your relationship ended, you were still in love with her." He didn't even miss a beat before he responded.

"Yeah." The one word was light and easy. There was nothing to deny, so he didn't even pretend.

"It's hard for me because I feel as though I might never measure up." Once the words fell out of my mouth I was both exhausted and relieved. Simultaneously. I'd never had a sentence take so much weight off my shoulders, and the tired feeling that came over me only emphasized how deeply I had been holding that truth in, how far down I'd had to dig to find it.

The quick and easy response he'd had just a moment ago did not come as easily that time. He was quiet for too long, making me nervous. When he finally did speak, it was soft words.

"I'm not going to lie and tell you that being with someone other than my wife was easy at first. That's why I hadn't dated anyone since she passed. It was a struggle for me, at first. Dealing with being attracted to someone else. It felt foreign and wrong. But running into you at Jaxy's school, feeling that connection, that was the first time I'd felt anything close to what I felt for Olivia."

It was hard listening to him speak; trying to make me feel better but not really saying anything to put my mind at ease. I wasn't sure if there was anything he could tell me that would make it easier, but he hadn't yet. I felt the distinct pinch in the back of my throat that told me tears were coming, and I didn't want to cry in his tub with his arms around me. If I was going to cry, I wanted to do it at my own apartment, in my own bed, where I could sob all I wanted without worrying about ugly crying in front of him.

"Do you understand me, Grace? A part of me died right along with Olivia, and I was almost certain it would be dead forever. But then I saw you and something inside me sparked alive again."

Oh, God.

"I'm not the same man I was with her. The man in love with you right now, the man whose arms are around you, he's not the same man who loved her. She's gone and he'll never be back. But I'm here, with you, right now."

My lip stung as I bit down on it, trying to keep in the sobs. The hurt in his voice cut right through me like a knife. The arm that had been wrapped around me moved, and his hand pulled my face up to look at him. His gaze pierced mine and his breath panted across my face.

"I'll admit, I hadn't given much thought to how difficult it might be to date me, how hard it would be to be the woman to follow Olivia, but you have to know that's not how it works. I'm not comparing anyone to anything. Does that make sense?" He was definitely asking me a question, but I didn't know the answer. It didn't make sense; I didn't understand. And I'm not sure I was meant to. "I'm not thinking about how she's gone, I'm thinking about how you're here."

"Devon" was all I could manage before his mouth was on mine. He kissed me with desperation, as though he was trying to persuade me with his mouth how much I meant to him, and I felt it, all the way down to my bones.

"Please don't question what I feel for you," he said against my lips between kisses. "I love you, Grace. I love what I see in our future. Death ends things in a way that is both final and also unfinished. My love for her never died, per se, but it changed after she was gone. But I love you now, and I want to love you forever. I don't want you thinking that you're not enough, because you're everything."

I had no words, so I just kissed him back. I twisted my body so that I was no longer lying back on him, but so that my chest was pressed against his, and he didn't miss a beat. His hands moved down my body, gliding easily over my skin, making water slosh against the side of the tub. One of his hands went down over my backside and the other came up, palming my breast.

My lips abandoned his to release a moan as his hands found every part of me.

I'd given him my words, and he'd given me his own.

We spent the next few hours using our bodies to communicate what we couldn't say with words.

Chapter Eighteen

Grace

The next two weeks passed without incident. We filed the restraining order and there were no more incidents at the bar. Summer vacation was coming to an end, and the kids were gearing up for their trip to California with Evie and Nate.

Things between Devon and I had improved, and even though I still struggled sometimes with insecurity, I knew it would only take time to overcome. Devon did nothing to make me feel unwanted; quite the opposite in fact.

Ever since our night in the tub, and the hours after in his bed, he'd done nothing but make me feel as though his relationship with me was at the top of his priority list. Besides his children, he was solely focused on me and making sure I was comfortable and happy.

I was. Blissfully so. And I worked hard to return the favor. I was at his house most nights, although I was still sneaking out before the kids woke up. There was a distinct joy that came with settling into a routine with him, Jax, and Ruby. I no longer felt as though I was visiting when I was at their house, but that there was a place carved out for me.

"Daddy." Ruby's angry voice carried down the hall.

"What?"

"My swimsuit is ruined."

"What do you mean?"

"Look."

Devon and I both turned our heads from the television and saw Ruby standing at the mouth of the hallway, holding up her one-piece swimming suit. It had holes cut in it, along with other wide strips of material missing.

"What in the world happened to it?" I asked.

"Jax?" Devon called, seeming to already know who was responsible. I tried to hide my smile as Jax emerged from his room, head bowed, guilt written all over his face. "Did you do this to your sister's swimsuit?"

"I needed something to make a slingshot with! The material of her suit was stretchy and I had to use it since I couldn't find a rubber band big enough."

"You used my swimsuit to make a slingshot?" Ruby yelled, obviously not finding the humor in the situation I was. She lunged toward him, but he was faster than her and ran away before she could catch him.

"Ruby," Devon called out, his voice sharp and swift. "I'll handle your brother. Don't lay a hand on him."

She huffed out a frustrated breath and stomped back down the hallway. Once she was out of earshot I buried my face in Devon's chest and let out the laughter I'd been holding in. His warm hand came to the back of my head, holding me to him, and I felt his chest rumbling with laughter too. I pulled back and looked him in the eye.

"Only Jax would cut up his sister's swimsuit to make a slingshot. He's crazy smart." My smile was wide. I'd been smiling a lot in the past few weeks.

"I don't know about that. Smart people usually consider the consequences before performing such obvious crimes. Did he not think he was going to be caught?" He let out another laugh, but when it died down it turned into a sigh. "A swimsuit trip was not on my agenda. Evie's coming to get the kids tomorrow and I have to work all day."

"I can take her to get a swimsuit," I said, moving my hand up his chest to rest on his shoulder. "I'd love to, actually."

"You have time tomorrow?"

"I'm free as a bird," I responded with a smile.

"You'd really be helping me out. Ruby's been a handful lately and I'm sure Jax doesn't want to go swimsuit shopping with his sister."

"It'll be good. I've had plenty of one-on-one time with Jaxy at school and stuff. It'll be nice to have a little girl time with Ruby. Maybe we can go get our nails done or something too." A sweet smile spread across his face and he leaned in, kissing me deeply until I was out of breath. "What was that for?" I asked when he pulled away.

His thumb came up and rubbed right under my bottom lip. "You called him Jaxy. I don't think I've ever heard you call him anything except Jax."

It hadn't occurred to me that I hadn't been using his nickname. I'd heard Devon and Ruby call him that ever since we started dating.

"I guess you finally rubbed off on me," I said, lifting one shoulder in a shrug.

"I think, perhaps, you finally are starting to feel like a part of our family."

"Perhaps," I whispered, emotions creeping back into my voice. Never in my wildest dreams had I imagined finding a man as wonderful as Devon and finding a place in a family. A family was all I'd ever dreamed about, and sitting here with him, his arms around me, children arguing down the hall, it all seemed too good to be true.

"I think you should stay here tonight." His words were definitive.

"All right," I agreed. It wasn't as though I hadn't stayed over almost every night in the last month.

"And I want you to be here when the kids wake up."

"Devon—" I began to argue, but he cut me off.

"I want you to get used to it as much as them. I promise it won't be a big deal. In fact," he sat up straighter with his words and then called out, "Kids, come out here for a moment."

"What are you doing?" Panic made my heart race.

He smiled at me in response, then pressed a quick kiss against my forehead before moving me off him and sitting up straight on the couch. Ruby and Jax came down the hallway, both with expectant looks on their faces.

"Quick family meeting," Devon started once both kids were in front of us. "We're all going to go out to dinner tonight, the four of us, and we're going to stop at Grace's on the way home. She's going to grab some of her stuff and she's going to stay the night here. Then, tomorrow, I'm going to take Jaxy to Grandma's like normal, but Ruby's going with Grace to get a new swimsuit and do some other girly stuff." My mouth gaped open and I stared at Devon as though he'd grown a second head. "Anyone have anything to say about any of that?"

"I wanna go do girly stuff too," Jaxy whined.

"Sorry, bud. You cut up your sister's swimsuit, you lose out on the fun stuff." There was a pause.

196 |The Presence of Grace

Devon gave a small clap of his hands. "Okay, as you were. We'll leave for dinner in a few hours. No more fighting or Grace and I will pick a really boring, grown-up place."

"Okay," both the kids said in unison before they turned and made their way back toward their rooms.

"See?" Devon said, turning to me. "Problem solved. Now everyone's on the same page."

I was speechless for a moment, my thoughts trying to catch up with everything that had happened in just a few minutes. "You're crazy," I said on a laugh. I wasn't laughing because I thought it was funny, I was laughing at how surprisingly he handled it, and how the kids didn't seem to bat an eye at the idea of me spending the night.

"I'm tired of losing time with you, Grace. Tired of watching you get up early and go home to a cold and lonely bed when there's no reason you can't stay here, with me, and be a part of this life. Unless you don't want to be...." His words trailed off as insecurity seeped into his voice.

"No. God, no. Of course I want to be here. You and the kids mean everything to me. I'm just worried about taking this too fast. What if we all get comfortable and a few months down the line something happens and we aren't together anymore."

His hands formed fists, the muscles in his forearms rippling from the tension.

"I refuse to live my life worrying about the future. I love you and you're not some woman I just met on the street. I *know* you, and I know how much you care about my kids, and we're all better off when you're here, with us."

I reached over and laid my hand on his arm, and let out a breath when he relaxed. He exhaled, the tension in his arms melting away, then his head dipped low and he turned to look at me. "I can't keep you away because I'm afraid of losing you. That doesn't make any sense to me."

"When you say it like that, it doesn't make any sense to me either." I leaned toward him, my side resting against him, my head tilting until it landed on his shoulder. "I'll try to stop worrying about everything. I want to be here. I do."

"Just let us love you." His words were pleading.

It's all I'd ever wanted.

"Okay."

There was no particular nail salon I favored, as regular manicures weren't really in a teacher's budget, but I figured one at the mall would be as good as any. Ruby and I had gone to a coffee shop and I'd gotten a chocolaty coffee drink with far too much sugar, and she'd ordered an Italian soda. We'd wandered through part of the mall on the way to the salon, but she was being particularly quiet. She didn't look so great either, if I was being honest. She was pale and she looked tired. I hoped she wasn't getting sick right before her trip to California.

When we'd walked into the nail salon, I helped her pick out a pale pink color for her nails and then decided to use the same one. We were ushered to chairs right next to each other and then the nail techs went to work on us.

"Are you excited for your trip?" I asked as the nice woman in front of me cut down my cuticles.

"Yeah, I'm just not looking forward to the plane."

"Flying isn't my favorite thing either. But that's why Evie's flying here, so she can ride back with you and Jaxy, so you aren't alone." I looked over at her, wondering if it was the stress of the flight that was making her look off. "You don't have anything to worry about, Ruby. Your father would never let you get on a plane if it weren't safe."

She gave me a small, unconvincing smile. "I know."

"Are you all right, honey? You don't look like you're feeling well."

"I'm okay, I think. I'm just really tired and I have a stomachache."

I took the hand that wasn't being worked on and pressed it against her forehead. "You don't feel warm."

She shook her head. "I don't feel like I'm sick. I just feel icky."

"I'm sorry, sweetie. Do you want to go home?"

"No," she answered softly. "It's okay. I was really looking forward to a girl day."

She said the words with a sad smile that broke my heart. I wrapped my arm around her and pulled her as far into me as I could without disrupting our manicures.

We spent the next half hour chatting quietly about her entering middle school, finally being at a school without her brother, and which boy band she'd fallen in love with over the summer. When our nails were dry we stood and as I went to pay she asked the tech if they had a restroom.

"I'll meet you up front," I said as she wandered to the back of the salon where the tech said the bathrooms were.

I paid and then took my phone out and started thumbing through my e-mails, catching up on some district communication from the school. It was boring, back-to-school business, but it took a few minutes to read through. When I got to the end, I realized Ruby had been gone a while and I debated whether I should check on her or not. I decided to give her a few minutes, but with each passing second she was gone, worry worked its way through me. Finally, I walked to the back of the salon, following the path I'd seen her take, to a door with a restroom sign on it.

I knocked gently and called out to her. "Ruby, are you in there?"

"Grace?" she asked, and my heart squeezed at her voice. She sounded panicked and scared. "Is that you?"

"Yes, sweetie, it's me. Are you all right?" I pressed my ear to the door, trying to grasp any tiny piece of information about what was bothering her. Had she gotten sick? Was she hurt? I heard sniffling, like she was crying, and I knocked more urgently. "Ruby, what's going on?"

Finally I heard shuffling, then the lock clicked, and the door opened just slightly. I saw Ruby's tearstained face and every instinct inside me went into overdrive. Something was wrong with her and I needed to fix it. She wouldn't meet my gaze, but after a moment she opened the door and took a step back, allowing me in.

I slipped into the bathroom, shutting and locking the door behind me, and then took a moment to look her up and down. She didn't appear to be hurt, but there weren't any other clues as to why she was upset.

"Ruby, can you tell me what's wrong?"

She finally looked up at me, but then burst into tears. She reached up to wipe the tears away, but I went straight to her and wrapped my arms around her, running my hand down her hair. I held her while she cried and I just kept praying she'd tell me what was upsetting her. Finally, the cries died down, but she didn't let go of me. A few moments later, she finally spoke.

"I think I started my period."

There were so many emotions blooming in my mind, it was hard to keep them all from overwhelming me. The first was relief; I was so glad there wasn't something more serious bothering her. The second was concern, then confusion, and then I just wanted to hug her.

So I did.

"Is this your first one, sweetie?" I asked gently, trying not to say the wrong thing. She nodded against my chest, and my heart just ached for her. Suddenly, everything fell into place: her stomachache, the fatigue, the general ickiness she felt. This would also be a huge reminder of the fact that her mother was gone. No matter how well Ruby and I got along, no matter how much she liked me, I could only think of how much she was probably missing her mother. I knew I could never replace her, but right then I vowed I would do everything to make this day easier for her.

"It's okay. Hey," I said, pulling away and cupping her wet face with my hands. "Everything is going to be all right. I know it's scary and probably not a lot of fun right now, but this is a magical day, Ruby. Today's the day you become a woman." I couldn't help the tears that stung my eyes and the pinching in the back of my throat. "I know it doesn't feel like it, but this is something to celebrate." I let out a little laugh.

The words were so true, but I hated getting my period. "You're part of an elite club now."

"An elite club?" she asked, her tone sardonic.

"Yes," I exclaimed. "Being a woman is a beautiful thing, and even though it sometimes sucks, you should appreciate all the things your body is capable of. You don't need to think about having kids for another ten or fifteen years, maybe even twenty, but this is just your body preparing itself for the most amazing feats."

"Amazing feats?" she parroted, still not buying into my spiel.

"Growing and birthing babies. It's the most amazing thing anyone will ever do with their body, and only women can do it, Ruby. It's a gift."

"It doesn't feel like a gift."

"I know. Most of the time it doesn't, but it is." My throat tightened again, thinking about the torture of still getting a period, my monthly reminder that my body was broken.

"Do you have anything at home? Pads? Midol?"

"My school gave out these little boxes that have three pads in them," she said.

"Well, that's not going to do the trick at all. You've got nothing else at home?"

She raised her eyebrows at me. "No. I haven't asked my dad to stock up on maxi pads just in case I started my period."

I laughed and ran my thumb under her eye, trying to dry the last of the tears.

"Fair point." She laughed with me. "Okay, new plan. We're headed to Target. We can get everything we need there. Do you still want to try on swimsuits?"

She thought about the question, and her face scrunched up, giving me my answer.

"Of course not. I wouldn't want to try on swimsuits while on my period either. Okay," I said with new enthusiasm. "We'll go to Target, get everything we need, then we'll pick out a few swimsuits you think you'll like, buy them, and then later tonight or tomorrow you can try them on at home. Keep whichever one you want and I'll return the rest." I ran my hands down the sides of her face, then rested them on her shoulders. "Sound like a plan?"

"Okay," she said softly. "But…," she started, then looked as though she was too embarrassed to continue.

"Hey, you can ask me anything, Ruby. Okay? Anything."

She took a breath then said, "What should I do right now? You know, about the blood."

"Right," I said, thinking. I had exactly one tampon in my purse, not ideal for an eleven-year-old. "Is there a lot? Has it leaked through your underwear onto your jeans?"

"No. Not yet. There isn't much."

"Okay, good." I walked to where the toilet paper was and pulled a bunch off, wrapping it around my hand until there was a thick pad. "I'm going to step outside and I want you to put this in your underwear. Do you know where it goes?" She nodded but didn't say anything. "This will be fine for the drive to Target. As soon as we get there, we'll buy everything we need and then get fixed up in the bathroom. Don't worry. Every woman has faced this dilemma. You are not alone." I handed her the toilet paper pad, then made my way out of the bathroom, giving her my best smile before I shut the door behind me. I heard the lock click into place and I leaned against the wall, letting out a deep breath I hadn't realized I'd been holding.

After a few quiet minutes, Ruby finally emerged from the bathroom.

"Good to go?" I asked, putting a smile on, trying to communicate that everything was going to be all right.

"Yeah," she said, although she didn't look too convinced.

We walked out to the car and I could tell she was tense. I totally understood. Any woman would understand the dreaded walk through a public place when you weren't properly equipped with suitable period protection. It was horrifying and embarrassing all at the same time—no matter your age.

We made it to the car and she slid in with a sigh of relief.

"Everything will be fine, Ruby. Promise." She gave me a weak smile, but I could tell she didn't believe me. At least, not yet. "I was eleven when I got my first period too." I wasn't sure why I'd offered that information, but I figured anything I could tell her at this point to make her feel like less of a leper would do her some good.

"Yeah, same as you. Although, I had already started sixth grade and was in school when it happened."

Ruby gave me a horrified look.

"Unlike you, I hadn't had any symptoms. No stomachache, no fatigue. And the worst part was, I had no idea I'd even started. The bell rang between classes and I left one class to go to the other and didn't realize I had a big bloodstain on the back of my pants."

"Oh, my goodness," she said, obviously disturbed by my story.

"Right? And I walked all the way through the school before a teacher grabbed my arm and whispered in my ear that I needed to go see the school nurse." I remembered the day so vividly and realized Ruby would probably remember today much the same way. I wanted to make sure it wasn't horrible. "I had to wear a saggy pair of sweatpants the rest of the day with a giant pair of underwear the nurse had given me."

We were both quiet for a moment, then Ruby said, "I guess it could have been worse. I could have been out somewhere with Dad and Jax."

I tried to contain my laughter at the mental image popping into my brain. "Your father loves you very much, but you're right—he probably would have freaked out."

Ruby sank down farther into her seat. "Ugh, I can't imagine having to tell him about this."

"Listen, I don't want to promote you keeping things from your father, because I'm sure he'd want to know about this, but it isn't necessary for you to run home and tell him right away. I mean, I'll get you enough stuff to keep you stocked for a while, but you can always come to me if you're uncomfortable talking to your dad."

Again, she was quiet for a few moments before she spoke. "It's not that I don't want him to know, I just can't imagine telling him. Like, I don't really want to talk to him about it. Ever."

I laughed because I understood. When I was eleven, I would never have told my dad about my period. I was sure my mom took care of that.

"Do you want me to tell him?"

"You wouldn't mind?" she replied, as if she were asking so much of me. My heart leapt at the idea of her trusting me to tell her father.

"Of course not, Ruby. I'd do anything for you. And your brother. You guys have to know that."

"Thanks," she replied shyly, and I felt some of the tiny cracks in my heart seal up, filled in by this girl and her ability to let me be a part of her life. "But can you do it when I'm not around. And make sure Jax doesn't hear. The last thing I need is him bugging me about this."

"Done and done."

We pulled into the Target parking lot and I gave her a big smile. "Come on, time to get you stocked up."

The store wasn't terribly busy, which I was thankful for. It was about lunchtime and the middle of the week, and I was glad there wasn't anyone else in the feminine hygiene aisle when we arrived.

"Okay, so you're going to need two different kinds of pads to start, one for the day and one for the nighttime."

"Really?" she asked, looking overwhelmed.

"Yeah, but only because you roll around in your sleep, so you need something with a little more protection."

"Oh."

I grabbed the pads I thought would be best and tossed them in our cart.

"Now we need Midol."

"What about tampons?"

"Tampons are more for older girls. Maybe when you're fifteen or sixteen."

"Why do I have to be older? What's the difference?"

"Well, pads just sit in your underwear, and tampons actually go inside your body. It's better to wait until you're older before trying them." I prayed she took my answer and didn't pry any more. I didn't want to explain hymens and tampon usage to her in the middle of Target.

"What's Midol for?"

"Midol is medicine for women and it's specially made to treat the symptoms of your period."

"So it's different than just Tylenol?"

"Yeah. And you don't have to take anything if you don't want to, but it's nice to keep around just in case you need it."

"Like if I get cramps?"

"Yeah."

I found the Midol and threw it in the cart, then headed toward the clothing. We picked out a new package of underwear and a few swimsuits she liked, and then I pushed my cart toward the ice cream and threw a few cartons in as well.

"We'll need that later," I promised.

As we headed toward the checkout, I tried to impart all my womanly knowledge. "Always look for a woman cashier if you're embarrassed to buy pads. You shouldn't be—it's a part of life for everybody—but it's okay if you are. If there's a woman working, go to her line. If you can't find a woman, find an older man, they usually know what's up." We found a nice woman who rang up all our items and even though Ruby looked embarrassed and as red as a tomato, the woman never gave away whether she'd figured out our situation. I felt for Ruby though and remembered those moments where you were sure everyone on the planet knew you were on your period. After I paid, I took her to the restroom and was glad to see the private family bathroom was available. I took her in, got her situated, explained how the pad adhered, then I stepped out to let her take care of it.

A few minutes later, a shy and slightly embarrassed Ruby emerged.

"Everything all squared away?"

"I think so," she said with a shy smile.

"All right." I took the bags from her and we walked out to the car. As I buckled I said, "I'm supposed to take you to your grandparents' house now, but if you'd rather go home and watch movies and eat ice cream, I could be persuaded to extend our girls' day."

Finally, a genuine smile appeared on her face and I couldn't help but smile back.

"That would be awesome," she said enthusiastically.

I grabbed my phone and dialed Devon's number.

"Hey, babe," he said as a greeting, making my pulse speed up. "How'd girls' day go?"

"It went fine, although Ruby's not feeling so great at the moment, so I thought I'd take her back to your house instead of to your parents'. Would that be all right?"

"Of course. Is she all right?"

"She'll be fine, just a little under the weather. Do you think you could let your mother know not to expect her?"

"Sure. Can I talk to Ruby?"

"Yeah, here she is."

I handed the phone to her, giving her a supportive smile.

"Hey, Dad." She paused and I could hear Devon's voice through the phone, though I couldn't make out what he was saying. "No, I'm okay, I just don't feel well." She tucked a loose strand of hair behind her ear and gave me another smile. "I will, Dad. Okay. Here you go. Love you too."

She handed the phone back to me and I put it up to my ear.

"Everything all right?" I asked.

"Yeah, just wanted to get a feel for what's wrong."

"Don't worry. I'll take good care of her until you get home."

"I know you will. And thank you."

"Nothing I'd rather be doing today," I said, giving Ruby a wink. "See you later."

"Love you, Grace."

His words halted me. We'd never said those words so blatantly to each other, never over the phone, and definitely never in front of his kids. He knew I was with her, and yet he'd said the words and was waiting for a response.

"Grace," he said again, his voice lower this time. "It's okay. My kids know how I feel about you. If they can't tell by the way I smile when I'm around you, then they picked up on it by the fact that you're always around and always making me happy. It's okay to love me in front of my children."

I sucked in a deep breath, reeling from the whiplash of looking forward to cookies 'n' cream ice cream with a tween movie to facing a monumental moment in my relationship.

"I love you, Grace," he repeated. I took in a breath and answered him as best I could.

"I love you too, Devon."

"I'll see you when I get home. Take care of my girl."

"Always," I said before I could think better of it. I dropped my hand with the phone in it and ended the call. Then, I gave a tentative look at Ruby and, sure enough, she was looking right at me, but I couldn't read her expression.

"Thanks for everything today, Grace," she finally said once we were on the road.

"Anytime, Ruby. I'm glad I was with you and you weren't alone."

"I'm glad you're here, too."

Chapter Nineteen

Devon

My day had been one long battle. I worried about Grace and Ruby and how they'd get along together, then I worried when Grace had called telling me Ruby was sick, and then the traffic to the airport prevented me from picking up Evie on time, which made me late getting Jax. So when we finally arrived home, I was stressed and perhaps a little bit grumpy.

Most of that grumpiness faded away when I saw Grace and Ruby in the living room together. They were both on the couch, leaning in toward the center and each other, each with a big blanket—even though it was ninety degrees outside—and there was evidence of ice cream consumption on the coffee table. I recognized *Pitch Perfect* on the television and knew it was Ruby's favorite even though I found it a little too mature for an eleven-year-old. She loved it.

Something about the image of Grace and Ruby spending time together made the lump of tension inside me melt away.

"Hey, there're my girls," I said as I stepped inside, carrying Evie's one, small overnight bag. "How're you feeling, Ruby?"

She shrugged and said, "I'm okay." I wasn't particularly convinced by her answer, but I looked to Grace and she was smiling, so I figured everything was all right for the moment.

"Glad to hear it." Evie stepped in behind me and Ruby's face lit up.

"Aunt Evie!" Ruby jumped up from the couch so quickly, all my doubts over her health slipped away.

I watched as Evie and Ruby embraced, then turned my attention to Grace, who was rising from the couch. I made my way over to her, my hand wrapping around the curve at her waist and pulling her to me gently.

"Everything all right? With Ruby?"

"Yeah," she replied softly. "Everything's great." She smiled and wrapped her fingers in my shirt, gripping me like she didn't want me to ever let her go, and I didn't plan on it. I leaned forward and pressed a kiss against her lips. It wasn't obscene, but it was more than just a peck. I wanted so much more, but was reminded of the other people in the room when I heard Evie talking to the kids.

"Nate is so excited to see you guys tomorrow! He bought us all matching Disney shirts."

"Why didn't he come with you?" Jaxy asked.

"He had a few things to finish up in Fairbanks, so he's going to meet us at the airport tomorrow since his flight comes in an hour before ours. But he's really looking forward to spending some time with you."

I watched Jaxy bounce with excitement, but Ruby looked more worried than anything else. Something was up with her. I was about to ask Grace again about Ruby, but the smell permeating the house caught my attention.

"Is something cooking?"

"Grace and me made lasagna." Ruby said the words proudly.

"You made dinner?" I asked Grace, looking back at her.

"You had a lot on your plate tonight, so I figured I'd make dinner so it would be ready when you got home."

It was the smallest and most insignificant thing, but it had been years since a woman had made dinner and had it ready for me when I came home. I didn't normally consider myself a caveman, but in that moment, there was nothing sexier than Grace making a lasagna.

"Hey, Grace, it's good to see you again." This came from Evie, who was walking toward us with Jaxy wrapped around her leg and Ruby still clinging to her middle. She held her hand out for Grace to shake, but Grace waved her away and hugged her on the side without any children attached.

"You, too. How was your flight?"

"Long," Evie said on an exhale. "But I got a lot of work done, so that's a bonus."

"Dinner will be ready in a few minutes and hopefully you can relax."

"It's smells amazing."

"Jaxy, take Evie to your room and show her where she's sleeping. And take her bag, too." Jaxy jumped at the chance to help and grabbed her bag, then pulled her down the hall. Ruby, still very much excited about Evie's presence, went with them. I took the opportunity of a few moments alone and brought Grace back in, wrapping one hand around her waist and using my other hand to grip the back of her neck, bringing her lips up to mine.

"You didn't have to make dinner," I said after I'd pulled away, and I loved the way her little breaths panted against my face.

"I know. I wanted to."

My eyes met hers and I couldn't help but just take her in, look at her while her body was wrapped up in my arms.

"I'm going to miss having you next to me tonight," I said, finally resting my forehead against hers. Even though I'd told her there wouldn't be a problem, she insisted on not sleeping here when Evie was staying. She claimed it made her uncomfortable, but I wanted her in my bed. Every night. The only consolation was I knew for the days the kids were in California, Grace would be in my bed and any other room I wanted her in. We'd both taken the weekend off and I planned on spending it indoors and naked.

"My neighbors probably think I've been kidnapped," she said with a laugh. "I haven't been in my own bed in so long. My plants are probably all dead."

"Well, you're all mine starting tomorrow."

"Looking forward to it," she said just before she kissed me again. We were interrupted by the timer on the oven. I groaned as she pulled away, but it was for the better, as both kids came running down the hallway at the thought of food.

"How about we eat on the deck tonight? It's not too hot."

"Sounds great," Evie said, coming out of the hallway. "I'll take all the fresh air I can get after that plane ride."

"Kids, set the table outside." I gave Grace a wink and then went to help the kids.

An hour later and the food was all gone, the wine was still flowing, and the sun was beginning to dip lower in the sky. Grace and Evie were chatting each other's ears off, and I was enjoying watching two women I cared very deeply about become friends.

I hadn't necessarily been worried that Grace and Evie wouldn't get along—it was hard to dislike either of them—but I knew there were reasons Grace could have kept her distance.

I loved that she didn't.

She took every opportunity to engage Evie and find out more about her, and Evie did the same in return. It made everything seem that much easier, that much more perfect.

The kids had brushed their teeth, put on their pajamas, and said lengthy good nights to all of us. Ruby took her time with Evie, but took even more time with Grace, thanking her for their day together. I walked both the kids back to their rooms and tucked them in, and when I came back out on the deck, I found Evie and Grace both laughing so hard they had tears streaming down their cheeks.

"Something tells me Evie is telling you embarrassing stories about me."

"I was just explaining that one time, at the lake my sophomore year, how you passed out drunk on the boat deck and your frat brothers spelled 'Kick Me' out on your back with sunscreen, and how you couldn't figure out for the rest of the weekend why everyone kept kicking you." Both the women burst into another fit of giggles at my expense, and I had to laugh along, because it was pretty funny. Now. Ten plus years later. It hadn't been so funny at the time.

Their laughter died down and both of them took sips of their wine, and then Grace spoke up.

"Since you're both here, I think there's something we should all talk about."

Evie gave me a worried glance, but then turned to Grace.

"What's on your mind?" I asked, but I wasn't sure I wanted the answer.

"Ruby asked me to tell you in private," Grace said, looking at me. "But, since she'll be with you a few days, I think it's important you know, too," she said, turning to Evie. Grace took in a deep breath and then continued. "Today, while Ruby and I were out having a girls' day, she got her first period."

Evie's mouth dropped open and her hand swiftly came up to cover it, her eyes darting to me.

"She what?" I asked, unclear on what she was saying. Disbelief was the main reason I needed her to explain again.

"She started her period," Grace replied gently, placing her hand on my knee.

"She's too young to start her period. She doesn't even have, you know," I motioned to my chest and then whispered, "boobs."

Evie was trying to hide a smile, but I could see it.

"She might not have impressive breasts, yet, but she's developing. And one doesn't really have much to do with the other as far as which comes first. It's not like a chicken and egg scenario. Plus, she's definitely old enough. I was eleven when I started mine."

"I was only twelve," Evie added.

"Whoa, whoa, whoa," I said, waving my hands in front of my face, resisting the urge to cover my ears. "I don't need graphic details."

"Trust us, Devon, those were hardly graphic details." Evie snorted and took another drink of her wine.

"I thought I had another four or five years."

"You thought she wouldn't get her period until she was sixteen?" Grace asked, clearly having underestimated how clueless I was about everything period-related.

"I don't know. Maybe I was just hoping I had more time. I am not prepared for this at all."

"Yeah, that's true. You need a trash can in your guest bathroom." This came from Evie.

"What? Why would you say that?"

"Because she's going to need to throw things in the garbage and she's not going to want to walk through the house with it balled up in her hand."

"Oh," I said quietly. "I hadn't thought of that."

"I took her out today and bought her everything she'll need for the next few months, but she's still pretty freaked out about the whole thing. She's afraid to swim, she's afraid to ride the rides at Disneyland, and she's really afraid that she'll leak on your sheets, Evie."

"Poor girl," Evie said with so much love in her voice.

"She said she wanted you to know, Devon, but she didn't want to tell you herself. I don't think she really wants to talk to you about it. I think she's embarrassed. Like we all were when we got our first period. Talking to our dads about it was the last thing we wanted, right, Evie?"

"Definitely."

"Olivia never got the chance to talk to her about this stuff. She was so young." The words slipped out of my mouth before I had a chance to think about them, but when my eyes found Grace, she wasn't upset. She just looked sad. Olivia was going to miss out on a lot of things, and that alone was upsetting, but the worst part was that Ruby and Jax were going to miss out on having those experiences with their mother. It was pure luck that Ruby had been with Grace that afternoon, and there was no doubt in my mind that Grace had made Ruby feel comfortable and safe in what was probably a stressful situation for her. What could have been a disaster, seemed to be a memorable day for my daughter and the woman I loved. When I walked in the house that evening, Ruby was obviously happy and not emotionally scarred, which was probably what would have happened had she been with me. Instead she had ice cream and a girly movie, and fluffy blankets on the couch. Grace had given her that. "Thank you for taking care of her today. It means more than I can even explain."

"Of course," she said softly. She looked as though she wanted to say more, but she didn't. She just gave me a smile.

"I'm glad you told me too, even though it's none of my business," Evie said.

"The way I figure it, Ruby needs as many women on her side as she can get. There's room enough for both of us."

If I hadn't already loved her, I would have fallen for her in that moment.

"I couldn't agree more," Evie said with a bright smile.

I wanted nothing more than to kiss Grace stupid, but since we had a guest, I decided instead to go make sure the kids were fast asleep, and maybe sneak a kiss to Ruby's forehead.

Chapter Twenty
Grace

Devon left Evie and me on the deck and I tried not to worry that it would become awkward. I'd known she was coming to stay for a night before taking the kids back to California, but I hadn't been sure how I would feel seeing her. The last time we'd been together, I'd had no idea about her previous relationship with Devon. The good news was I sensed absolutely no weirdness between us. In fact, I still really liked Evie. She was funny, smart, and it was obvious she really cared about the kids. There was no way to dislike her.

"Shelby mentioned she told you about my past with Devon."

Well, that was one way to start a conversation.

"She did. She did not, however, mention she'd spoken to you about it."

"I asked her not to. I didn't want you to be on the offensive when I saw you." Evie smiled at me and I couldn't help but smile back. "I love Shelby, she's great. I know you two are close, which, by the way, makes this the smallest universe ever." She laughed. "But there's no way Shelby can give you an accurate insight into the relationship I have with Devon."

"No, you're right. Shelby was concerned about me, knowing my history, but had nothing but great things to say about you. Devon filled in all the holes though, I think. I hope you aren't upset with Shelby. She didn't mean any harm."

"Oh, Grace," Evie said, waving her hand. "There isn't a vindictive bone in Shelby's little body. I knew she was just trying to look out for her friend. It says a lot that she would speak to both of us, ya know? She really just wants all of us to be happy, which leads me to my next point." She paused for a moment, but then took a deep breath and continued.

"Have you ever wanted something so bad, it was all you could see? You were so focused and so intent on that one thing that you were blind to everything else? And then one day, something different popped into your vision, and suddenly, that very thing you wanted so badly wasn't what you thought it was? Well, that was Devon. I loved him, in a way. But then Nate came along and changed all that. I'm not saying that what I felt for Devon wasn't real, it just wasn't what I thought it was. It was something, but it wasn't my everything. Nate is my everything."

All I could think about was Jeff. I'd like to think if I were still married and another man came along, I wouldn't bat an eyelash, but comparing Jeff and Devon was unfair to both of them. Jeff paled in that comparison, and I could only thank my lucky stars that Devon had come along, even if I had to endure a painful divorce to get to him. I hoped in the end it would all be worth it.

"I'll be really honest with you, Evie. I was really upset when I found out about your relationship with Devon. I knew there'd be complications getting involved with a widower with young children, but I love those kids and I was really up for the challenge. I hadn't anticipated competing with another woman." Evie tried to interrupt me, but I powered through, holding up a hand. "But I spoke about it with him and talked it through. And while I understand your relationship is complicated, I also understand it isn't romantic, even though at one time you both thought it might have been." She seemed to relax at my words. "If

I really thought Devon was romantically invested in another woman, I wouldn't be here."

"I'm glad to hear that. You're a wonderful woman and you deserve a great guy. And Devon is one of the best."

"I agree," I said with a smile. "The best thing for Ruby and Jax is if we're all friends, so that's what I'd like, but I'd like to be friends even if it weren't for the kids."

"To friendship," she said, raising her wine glass.

"To friendship." We clinked our glasses and took a sip.

"Olivia would have really liked you," Evie said after a few quiet moments.

Her words were unexpected, but the really unexpected part was my reaction to them. I hadn't ever considered what Devon's late wife would think of me, but the idea of her approval was overwhelming and I found tears welling in my eyes. I dabbed at my eyes, trying to maintain my composure, but felt compelled to speak.

"Even if it doesn't work out with Devon, and it's not meant to be with us, him and those kids deserve the best, Evie. They've been through too much to tolerate anything less. And frankly, I've had a pretty bad run myself. So, if they get even one tiny fraction of the happiness from me that I get from them, well, that's all I can ask for."

I watched as Evie dabbed away her own tears and then the sliding door opened and Devon walked out.

"Oh, no. Too much wine," he joked as he took his seat, making both Evie and me laugh through our tears.

"No such thing," Evie quipped.

I reached forward and clinked my glass against hers again, making Devon smile. I loved his smile. Especially when it reached his deep blue eyes and the little crinkles at the corners came out.

"I was just telling Grace that Olivia would have really liked her."

Devon went quiet for a moment, but his smile never faltered. Then he reached over and took my hand, threaded our fingers, and brought the back of my hand to his lips, leaving a kiss there.

"Yes, I do believe she would have."

"Really?" I asked, new tears stinging in my eyes. I didn't have a clue as to why the idea made me so emotional, but it did.

"Aw, come here, babe."

I rose up and took two steps to him, then sat on his lap, my arms winding around his neck, pressing my face to his chest, trying to keep the tears to a minimum.

"You don't have to cry," he said as he ran his hand up and down my back. "She would have loved you. And trust me, if she could pick anyone for me, it would be you."

"Stop," I said, sniffing against his chest.

"Okay," he said, laughing a little. "But you ladies have to lay off the wine. You can't drive home like this. I'll have to take you."

"Oh, no. I'm sorry. I didn't even think about that." I pulled back and wiped my tears, but Devon wouldn't let me get far and kept his arm wrapped firmly around my waist.

"It's not a problem. Evie's more than capable of being alone with my sleeping children for a half hour so I can drive you home."

"I don't mind one bit," she said with a firm nod of her head. "But before you go, I wanted to tell you both something. Well, Nate wanted to be here too, but that didn't work out." She took a breath and smiled widely. "We've picked a wedding date."

"Really?" I exclaimed. "When?"

"We want to have a Christmas wedding, in Hawaii."

"Oh my goodness! That's going to be beautiful!"

"That sounds amazing, Evie. I'm so happy for you," Devon said, gently putting me down and standing to hug her.

"Thank you," she said, hugging him back. "We want the kids to be in the wedding. Ring bearer and flower girl. Or maybe Ruby can be in the bridal party? I don't want to make her feel like a child."

"I think Ruby would love to be a part of your wedding in any way," Devon said.

"So, you'll come? Both of you?" Evie asked, her eyes darting between us.

"We wouldn't miss it for anything," Devon replied, hugging her again. When he pulled back, I moved to hug her too. There was so much happiness between all three of us, it almost felt like electricity in the air.

"Congratulations," I said as we hugged, meaning it with everything in me. Evie wasn't a threat to my relationship with Devon; I'd learned that. And if we'd met outside of those circumstances, I would have become fast friends with her.

"Thank you," she said as she pulled away.

"What kind of dress are you going to wear?"

"That's my cue to go get another beer," Devon said, laughing as he went into the house. Evie and I sat on the porch for another hour, looking at dresses and talking about venues, and there wasn't an ounce of awkwardness. Just the excitement of a new friendship.

Chapter Twenty-One

Devon

If I'd had any questions about Evie and Grace, they'd been put to rest. Nothing bonded women like wedding talk. The two women hugged at the door and said their good-byes before I walked Grace to my car and reluctantly drove her home for the evening.

Halfway to her house, her hand holding mine and resting in my lap, I turned to look at her.

"You know, you don't have to stay at your house just because Evie's in town for the night."

She shrugged. "It's okay. I don't mind. I didn't want to be in the way or anything. Plus, one houseguest is enough."

"You're not a houseguest, Grace. You're my girlfriend." Even in the darkness of the car, I could tell she was blushing.

"It's better this way," she said, giving my hand a squeeze. "The kids will get some great time with Evie."

"It's not you or her, Grace. They can get great time with Evie when you're there too. I know you're doing this because it feels right to you, but I just want you to understand that I don't want you to go anywhere. For any reason. I don't want you to feel like you're not welcome. I want you there. I want you with me."

"I love that you feel that way. And maybe next time I'll feel comfortable, but tonight it feels right to go to my own home. Evie's on your couch and it would feel awkward to sleep in your bed with someone down the hall."

I could understand her point, but it didn't make me feel any better about the situation. I'd gotten used to her in my bed and I wasn't looking forward to a night without her.

"The entire time the kids are gone, you're at my house. When you pack your bags in the morning, pack so you don't have to come back for anything. All right?"

"Bossy," she said with a smirk on her face.

"Damn straight," I said, bringing the back of her hand up for a kiss. "I'll come pick you up right after I drop Evie and the kids off at the airport tomorrow afternoon, and I'm not taking you home. I want you in my bed every night."

"Okay," she whispered, but I could tell she was smiling.

I pulled into her apartment complex, walked her to the door, and kissed her silly before she slipped into her home. I wanted nothing more than to follow her in and take her to bed, but I knew I had to bide my time. I stayed outside her door until I heard the dead bolt click, then made my way back to my car.

The kids were excited to fly to California, but I was still glad Evie was there to accompany them. Instead of a nervous good-bye, the kids were happy and practically vibrating with anticipation. The flight would be long, but they were armed with snacks, tablets, and books. I hugged and kissed both of them, told them to have the best time but to also be on their best behavior, and then I pulled Evie into a hug.

"Don't take any crap from them," I said with a laugh. "And make sure you tell Nate I said hello."

"I will," she said with a smile. "Don't worry about a thing. They're in good hands and we're going to have the best time."

"Disney World for spring break *and* Disneyland on summer vacation? I bet no one at school had a summer that cool," Jaxy said, smiling from ear to ear.

"I bet you're right."

Evie put her hand on my arm and angled me away from the kids.

"You have a good time too, okay?" she said, and then winked. "Enjoy the time without the kids. I know you'll miss them, but make sure you live it up without them. Go to a late movie, one that's R-rated, and eat all the junk food."

"Trust me, I've got plenty of adult activities planned."

"Good," she said with a laugh.

I watched them go through security and disappear around a corner, then let out a large sigh. I would miss them, but it was still a tiny relief to know they'd be gone a few days. Evie was more than capable of taking care of them. For three years I'd been doing it practically on my own, so I wasn't going to take this time for granted.

I had to stop a couple places to grab some supplies, but then I was going to pick up Grace and spend a few days enjoying her.

Chapter Twenty-Two
Grace

Devon meant business when he said I wasn't allowed to leave his house while the kids were away. When he picked me up, he took me straight there. He opened the door and motioned for me to walk in first, and I was greeted by four bouquets of one dozen roses each, one red, one pink, one purple, and one white. He said there was a dozen roses for each month since we'd met for the second time.

There was champagne, strawberries, and then there was Devon. He'd gone out of his way to give me a romantic evening, but all I'd needed was him.

For two days he held me captive.

Two gloriously wonderful and sexy days.

But eventually I convinced him we needed to leave the house and get some fresh air.

We went to a movie.

We went out to dinner.

We went on a champagne cruise around the marinas and coastline, all the while Devon's hands never left my skin. He was either holding my hand, grabbing my waist, or pulling me into his side with a strong arm around my shoulders. He wanted me near and I wanted the same thing.

At night he made love to me, telling me over and over how much he loved me, how glad he was we'd found each other again, and how he couldn't see his life without me in it. He held me close, spooning me as we slept, and made love again to me in the morning.

We video chatted with the kids every day, and I loved hearing about how much fun they were having with Evie and Nate, how exciting it was to be at Disney again, and all the rides they enjoyed. What made me smile the most though was how they seemed just as excited to talk to me as they did to Devon. They told me they missed me, and I with tears threatening told them how much I missed them too.

Talking to them made me emotional and on the second day I broke down.

"What wrong, babe?" Devon asked as soon as we hung up.

"I'm not sure. I just miss seeing their faces and talking to them, I guess. I miss the way Jaxy irritates Ruby and how Ruby rolls her eyes at you," I said through a mixture of laughter and cries.

"Ah, baby, I miss them too. They'll be home soon."

He said the word home like it included me, and deep down I hoped it would.

The day the kids were supposed to fly home was lazy. Devon went in to work, kissing me soundly before he left, grumbling about how the last night of an empty house had passed, but I remained in his bed, soaking up one of my last free days before I would have to go back to work at the school. I picked up a book I'd been trying to read all week, but hadn't because Devon wouldn't let me get a minute to myself. I smiled at the memory of him ripping the book from my hands and throwing it across the room before rolling me onto my back and keeping me otherwise occupied.

Without shame or regret, I stayed in his bed reading for hours.

I knew I'd have to get up eventually, but those hours were precious. The plan was for Devon to pick the kids up at the airport when he got off work. After their first flight, both the kids felt comfortable flying home on their own, so all the adults figured it would be okay to save Evie the time and the money, and let them fly as unaccompanied minors.

My phone rang an hour before their flight was to come in. I smiled when I saw it was Devon.

"Hey, you on your way to the airport?"

"Not quite," he said, sounding frustrated.

"What's wrong?"

"My mom was sick yesterday, and now my dad is sick, so there's no one here to watch the store. Usually, I'd just close up early and call it a day, but the computer system crashed and the software company's customer service line is only open for a few more hours."

I sat up from the bed and started looking for my shoes.

"I'll go get the kids, it's no problem."

"I appreciate that, but when Evie took them to the airport she gave them my name so no one else can get them now. I called the airline and checked. Only the person who was listed can pick them up, and I have to show ID."

"Oh, well, that sucks for us at the moment, but I understand. It's a good call on their part."

"Yeah."

"How can I help?"

"Do you think you could meet me at the airport? I'll get the kids off the plane, then you can take them home while I go back to the store to try and get the computer system put back together."

"Of course. I'll leave in just a minute."

Devon let out a sigh of relief.

"You know, I've done this for three years by myself, and I love you for a lot of reasons, but right now I love you for just being there. You'll never know how much your help and support means to me."

"Hopefully you'll never have to do it by yourself again," I said softly, letting all my insecurities take a back seat. It made me indescribably happy that Devon called me when he had a problem and wanted me to help him fix it. It had been a long time since I'd felt like someone's partner, or like someone needed me.

"Not if I have anything to do about it," he replied. "I love you, baby. I'll meet you at the baggage claim at the airport."

"Okay, I love you too."

When I saw Devon round the corner by the baggage claim, my face lit up. Then, from behind him, Jaxy came running toward me, arms outstretched and smile wide.

"Grace!" he exclaimed as he lunged for me. "I got to sit in the cockpit!" His arms wrapped around my waist and his face burrowed into my belly. I leaned down and squeezed him hard, thankful to be able to hug him again. He leaned back, but just his head, and looked up at me. "They said maybe next time I could help fly the plane!"

I laughed, but chose to go along with it. "Sounds amazing!"

"He kept asking them a million questions about flying so I think they just told him that to make him stop," Ruby said, trying to sound annoyed, but I could tell otherwise when she reached out and ruffled his hair.

Ruby stepped up next to me and wrapped one arm around my back, giving me a side hug. I wrapped my one arm around her shoulders and pulled her closer, pressing my cheek against the top of her head.

"Hey," I said to her softly. "How'd it go?" I asked the question quietly, not wanting to embarrass her in front of the boys by talking about her period. "Any issues?"

She looked up at me and smiled. "Nope. It was gone by the time we went to Disney." A smile broke out across her face and then she leaned into me again.

My eyes met Devon's as I had both his children wrapped in my arms and he mouthed, "I love you."

All I could do in response was pull his children closer and mouth back, "Thank you."

With their bags loaded into my car and the kids buckled into my backseat, Devon kissed me soundly on the lips and said he'd be home as soon as he could.

The drive home was filled with story after story of their time in California, all the fun things they'd done with Evie and Nate, and how they couldn't wait to visit again next summer. I sat quietly and listened, loving the way they were sharing everything with me, uncensored, without thinking. They trusted me and wanted to share things with me, and that made me unreasonably happy. Happier than I'd been in a very long time.

Along the way, I happened to notice a small white car make a really quick lane change behind me, squeezing in where there was hardly any room. The white car's driving made me nervous, so I sped up to put some distance between us. For the rest of the way to Devon's house I noticed the white car made all the same turns I did. By the time we were on the outskirts of their neighborhood, I was starting to worry.

When I pulled into Devon's driveway, I watched as the white car drove past. I let out a breath of relief when it turned at the end of the block, but my pulse was still racing.

Jaxy and Ruby climbed out of the car, arguing about who got control over the television remote first, as I went to the trunk to unload their bags.

"Ruby, will you please go unlock the door and leave it open so we can get everything inside?" I said, handing my keys to her.

"Sure," she said with a smile.

I opened the trunk and grabbed Jaxy's tiny suitcase that had Ninja Turtles on it and handed it to him.

"Here, Jaxy, take this inside. And if you could, before you fight over the TV with your sister, take all your dirty clothes to the laundry room so I can start a load."

"Okay," he said, happily taking his Ninja Turtle suitcase from me.

Just then I saw the same white car coming back toward the house. Panicking, all I could think of was getting the kids inside.

"Jaxy," I said, trying to keep the sudden terror from my voice but doing a horrible job. "Go inside and lock the door. Do not let your sister come out. Call your father and tell him to come home immediately."

"What?" His eyes were round with worry and confusion.

"Jaxy, baby, you have to do as I say." I looked over and saw the white car coming closer still. "Go inside. Now!" He ran from me, terrified, and my heart hurt for scaring him, but I had to keep him safe. The white car pulled to a stop across the street and I watched as the door opened and a man got out. Distantly, I heard the door lock behind me and Ruby yelling at Jaxy, trying to figure out what was going on, and the only thing I could think was that I was the last thing standing between whoever it was in the white car and those kids.

As the man stepped closer, I finally recognized him and my heart stopped cold.

"I only want to talk," he said, now in the middle of the street, walking straight toward me.

"I have a restraining order against you. You're not supposed to be within fifty feet of me. You need to leave."

"Not until you listen to me." His hand was in the pocket of his hoodie and the thought of what he could have in it made a huge lump form in my throat. My eyes were glued to his arm where his hand disappeared into the black fabric, but he kept talking. "Listen, this is all just one big misunderstanding. I'm not a criminal. I don't deserve to go to jail."

"You should have thought about that before you assaulted me behind the bar."

"I don't even remember that!" he screamed at me, moving even closer, his body jolting and jumping erratically. I heard more yelling from inside the house and all I could hope was that the kids would stay inside. "I was drunk! I'm not some scumbag who'd rape someone behind a bar." One of his hands came up to run through his hair, but halfway through his fingers gripped it and he tugged. "There's just so much pressure," he said, coming closer still. I took a step back but he just continued forward. "I'm supposed to graduate this year, get a job, be the successful businessman my father is, but I can't do what my father does. I can't *be* my father. I hate him."

My eyes kept glancing at his hoodie, hoping and praying he kept his hand in there, for fear of what he was holding.

"If I get charged with assault, my father will disown me," he said as if it were explanation enough. As though at his words I should just shrug and say, "Oh, well why didn't you say that in the first place?"

But I didn't say anything. I just took another step back, silently cursing when the back of my legs hit the bumper of my car. I was effectively trapped.

He came closer and my breathing quickened. I had nowhere to go and I had no idea what was in his pocket. I feared the worst, scenarios running through my mind. Would he shoot me? Stab me? Would Devon get here in time? Would the kids find me dead? All thoughts caused a whirlwind in my brain. My lungs worked overtime. Suddenly, there were spots, and my vision was spinning.

The last thing I saw was the man coming closer and standing over me, pulling his hand from his pocket.

Then everything went black.

Chapter Twenty-Three
Devon

"Daddy? Please come home. Fast. There's a man outside. He was in a white car, and he's talking to Grace and she looks scared." My blood chilled in my veins at the sound of Ruby's voice, scared and worried, and my heart thumped wildly in my chest. I didn't think. I just moved.

"Call 911. Now, Ruby. Stay in the house. Do not go outside. Do you hear me?"

"Daddy, I'm scared," she whispered. I jumped in my SUV and drove recklessly from the parking lot.

"Ruby, listen to me. Call 911 and give them our address. Stay inside. I'm on my way. Everything will be all right." I said the words even though I had no idea if I'd end up being right, but nothing would ever wipe away the memory of Ruby's voice crying over the phone, telling me she was scared, and I'd do or say anything in that moment to make her feel safe. Ruby had been through a lot. Hell, both my kids had, but fear was not something they'd had to deal with a lot. So to hear her scared, and be miles away, was not something I'd get over easily.

The five minutes it took me to drive to my house were the scariest five minutes of my life. I had no idea if Grace was okay or if my kids were okay, but I was driving like a madman to get to them.

When I pulled up to the house, I didn't see a white car. It could have been there, but I wasn't looking for it. My gaze was locked on Grace, lying on the ground with a pool of blood around her head.

I threw the car in Park, not bothering to turn it off, and ran to her. As soon as I was on the ground next to her and saw her chest move up and down with a breath, I let out my own breath of relief.

"Daddy!" I heard Ruby cry from the front door.

"Are you and your brother all right?" I asked, and she nodded, tears streaming down her face. "It's okay, sweetie. Everything's fine. Did you call 911?"

"Yeah," she cried. It was then I heard the faint sound of sirens in the distance.

"Stay in the house. Everything's going to be all right."

The ambulance and police cars showed up, sirens blaring, but the noise did nothing to rouse Grace. I sat with her until the paramedics pushed me away, but the whole time I was right there, telling her I loved her and that she wasn't alone.

When they loaded her into the ambulance, I wanted so badly to go with them, but knew I had to stay with the kids. I watched the ambulance pull away and then ran to the house to comfort my children, who were standing at the door, watching the scene unfold with tears in their eyes.

I managed to calm them down, but explained that we had to go to the hospital to be with Grace. Neither one of them argued and they practically ran to the car, ready to go and make sure she was all right.

We sat in the waiting room—waiting being the operative word. We'd been *waiting* for almost two hours with no updates. My mom came to the hospital even though she still wasn't feeling well, but my dad was in no condition. He kept calling, asking for updates, and I heard my mother whispering to him about how terrible I looked, how worried I was, and how upset the children were. My mother offered to take them back to my house to wait, but both Ruby and Jax refused—they wanted to see Grace.

Detectives hovered around us, trying to blend in with the noise and commotion of the emergency room, but looked out of place. They'd questioned the kids and myself, but none of us really had much to say. I explained what had happened at the bar, that perhaps the same man had been the one in the white car, but the weight of uselessness was heavy. I had nothing to offer them. Only Grace would be able to tell them exactly what had happened.

Every time the doors that led back to the emergency room opened, my eyes darted there and hope rushed through me, but no one had come for me yet. I'd asked the nurse working at the admin desk for information a hundred times, but she wouldn't tell me anything because Grace and I weren't family.

I wanted to scream at her that Grace was a part of me; that just because we didn't have the same last name yet didn't mean she wasn't everything to me, but I managed to keep my cool and take a seat. It didn't stop me from asking every ten minutes though.

Finally, the doors opened and a nurse I hadn't seen yet called out, "Devon Roberts?"

I stood immediately and walked toward her. "I'm Devon Roberts," I said urgently. "Is she okay?"

"Come with me" was all she said, and she turned around, heading back into the emergency room.

I grunted in frustration, but followed. We turned down a few different hallways and at each door we passed my eyes looked in, searching for Grace. Eventually, the nurse stopped at an open door and motioned for me to go in first.

When I walked in, all I saw was Grace lying in a hospital bed, an IV hooked up to her arm and a monitor beeping next to her bed. She had dark circles under her eyes, but she was breathing and her heart was beating. That was all I could ask for. Walking to the side of her bed, I picked up the hand that wasn't hooked up to anything and kissed her palm. At the touch of my lips, her eyelids began to flutter and slowly open.

"Grace?" I asked gently.

"She'll probably still be a little groggy, but she's okay," the nurse said, typing something into the computer next to Grace's bed.

"Grace, baby?" I said again, smoothing her hair out of her face. Her eyes opened again and I'd never seen a blue I liked more than the color of them right then.

"Hey," she whispered after she'd blinked a few times.

"Hey," I said back to her, kissing her hand again. "How are you feeling?"

"I'm okay." Her voice was quiet and I got the impression it was because she was weak and not because she was trying to keep the volume down. I leaned forward and kissed her forehead.

"You scared me," I whispered against her skin.

"I'm sorry. I was scared too."

"What happened?" I watched as her eyes closed and she took a breath, then she swallowed, and looked up at me.

"I thought a car was following us home. I watched it make all the same turns as me, but when I pulled in the driveway, it kept going. But after we all got out, it came back," she said, her voice shaking. "I told the kids to lock themselves in the house. Are they okay?" Her voice filled with panic and she winced as she tried to sit up, practically climbing out of the bed with worry.

"They're fine, I promise. They're worried about you, but they aren't hurt."

"I was so scared." She cried in earnest and nothing was going to stop me from crawling up beside her and holding her as she did. "I was so afraid something would happen to Ruby and Jax, and I don't know what I'd do."

I tried my best to soothe her, but I knew exactly why she was upset and knew how petrifying it could be to think about bad things happening to children, especially children you loved liked Grace loved my kids.

"They're fine," I said.

"But something could have happened. I don't remember anything. They were in the house, that man was standing there begging me not to press charges, and then I was waking up in the emergency room. He didn't go near the kids at all?" she asked, her eyes darting up to mine, looking for some reassurance.

"No, Grace, no one touched them. I promise." She let out a sigh of relief.

"Hi, Ms. Richards, I'm Dr. Miller. I was the attending on duty when you came into the emergency room this afternoon. How are you feeling?"

"My head still hurts a little, and I'm really tired."

He nodded, then his eyes darted over to me.

"Before we talk any further about your injuries, I want to make sure you're comfortable with your visitor being in the room. There are privacy laws that protect you—"

"Oh, it's fine to talk in front of Devon."

I gave her hand a squeeze again.

"What do you remember from your accident?" the doctor asked.

"Not a lot. I remember standing in the driveway and I was really scared, and then all of a sudden I got really tired, or woozy, I guess. And then I saw dark spots, and the next thing I knew I was waking up in the emergency room."

"Hmmm. Well, the police are going to want to talk to you about what happened, but as far as we can tell, it appears you passed out and hit your head against the concrete upon impact. We didn't have any real information when you were brought in, so we ran some tests to try and determine what was wrong. It's a good thing we did because otherwise we would have taken you to get some X-rays, which wouldn't be good for the baby."

"The what?" Grace asked, her voice shaky and weak.

"The baby. You're pregnant. Based on the hCG levels, you're probably only about two weeks along. Congratulations."

I looked down at Grace and her eyes flashed up to mine, wide with surprise and disbelief.

"But, I can't…. I've never…." Her words were falling from her mouth quickly, but I could tell she wasn't able to process a full sentence.

"She's been told before she can't get pregnant naturally."

"Listen, I'm no obstetrician, but I can tell when a woman is pregnant, and you definitely are."

"This can't be happening," she murmured. "I don't feel pregnant. I haven't been sick or anything."

"Like I said, it's very early. It probably wouldn't even show up on an over-the-counter test. But blood tests don't lie. It's too early for morning sickness. Give it about three weeks and you'll be sick as a dog." The doctor gave her a smile, but she just looked at him like he was speaking a foreign language. "However, this would explain the fainting. Some women experience fainting spells as a symptom of pregnancy. If it continues, you need to bring it up with your obstetrician. But seeing as how you were in a particularly stressful situation, the pregnancy could explain the fainting. Nothing else showed up on any of our tests to cause any concern."

"No, there's some mistake," Grace stammered, blinking rapidly and looking confused. "Maybe you have someone else's tests results mixed up with mine. Run the test again. I'm telling you I can't get pregnant. My ovaries don't even work. Please," she begged, her voice wavering, "just run the test again."

The doctor's eyes caught mine.

"Could you please run the test again?"

He shrugged and walked to the computer, typing away, telling the nurse to run the test again.

Grace curled toward me, pulled my hand to her chest, and began to cry quietly. I ran my free hand over her hair, avoiding the area on the back of her head that was stitched up, trying to offer any kind of comfort I could.

All the while my mind was running a million miles an hour.

A baby?

Grace was pregnant?

And why was Grace not thrilled to hear she was pregnant? She seemed so upset. Obviously, it was a shock. Was she in shock? Suddenly, *I* was feeling weak. I looked behind me and saw a chair so I pulled it to the side of the bed, never letting go of Grace's hand, and took a seat.

A baby.

With Grace.

So many emotions were warring for attention in the moment. I was scared, worried, confused, and surprised. But the loudest emotion, the one that was pulling rank on all the others, was elation.

"Everything is going to be all right, Grace. I promise." I just kept whispering words of comfort to her, stroking her hair, rubbing her back, and she continued to softly cry. She cried while the nurse took her blood, she cried while we waited for the results, and she cried when the doctor came back in and confirmed what he'd said before.

Grace was pregnant.

Chapter Twenty-Four
Grace

Detectives took my statement and told me the man who'd shown up at my house was being charged with violating an injunction which was automatic since I'd had a restraining order against him. The guy had been found circling the neighborhood while the cops were still on-scene, stopped, questioned, and then taken into custody.

He'd also been armed.

The thing he was holding onto in his pocket had, indeed, been a handgun.

That got him an extra charge of attempted aggravated assault with a deadly weapon. The detective told me the man had crumbled when interrogated and confessed. He also said he'd be in jail for a while, hoping that would ease my fears. And it did to a certain extent.

They'd released me from the hospital the next day after holding me one night for observation. Devon hadn't left my side once.

Prescription in hand for pain meds that were safe for the baby, the doctor told me to make an appointment with my obstetrician in the next four to six weeks. They said the stitches would dissolve, but that I needed to have the wound on my head checked in seven to ten days. They told Devon to keep an eye out for signs of a concussion.

I listened to everything they said, but absolutely could not comprehend any of it.

I was pregnant.

Pregnant.

Me.

Clearly, it was some sick joke.

I was silent the entire way home.

So silent and so out of it, I didn't even realize it wasn't my home we were going to. Devon had driven me back to his house. He opened the car door for me, took my hand as I climbed out, and led me to the front door, not saying a word. He opened the front door, walked me in, and took me back to the bedroom, where I sat on the edge of the bed.

"Where are the kids?" I managed, noticing we were alone.

He looked surprised to hear my voice.

"They went home with my mom."

"But your parents are sick."

"They've got a bug, baby. They'll survive. It's you I'm worried about."

"They were really scared, Devon," I whispered.

"They were scared for you. They were afraid you were hurt. But they saw you were all right, and I feel like you need a minute, or a night, to let your brain catch up with what's happening."

My eyes finally sought his out, and when they connected, they filled with tears.

"I'm so sorry," I cried, the lid finally popping off the container I'd been stuffing my emotions into.

"Sorry for what?" Devon asked as he sat next to me and wrapped his arms around me, pulling me to him.

"For everything," I sobbed. "I'm sorry that man came here, that I put your children in danger. I'm sorry

Anie Michaels | 245

I've made such a mess of everything, and now that doctor thinks I'm pregnant and I'm sorry because even if I am, it won't last, Devon. I'm not supposed to be able to get pregnant, so this is a mistake. And I'm sorry, so sorry, to bring you into this at all."

"Grace," he said as I collapsed against him, "you need to calm down." Just like he had all day, he ran his hand along my hair, and I had to admit it was soothing, but there wasn't any amount of comforting he could provide that would take away all the fear tearing me apart.

"It wasn't supposed to happen like this, Devon. I wasn't ever supposed to accidentally get pregnant. I'm so sorry."

"Grace, I was there too. We both made the decision not to protect against pregnancy, together. This is something we're in together, 100 percent. I don't want you carrying this weight on your own, because you're not alone. I'm right here."

"You aren't upset that I'm pregnant?" I asked, looking up at him.

"No, Grace. I'm not upset. Shocked? Yes. Surprised? Definitely. But I'm not upset. How can I be? I love you and somehow we made a baby against all the odds. We defied all the doctors who told you you'd never conceive, and our love made a baby. How could I be upset about that?" His hand came to cradle my face and he kissed me so softly it almost made me cry harder.

"I know he did two tests, but I just can't believe it. I've got this sick feeling in my stomach that it's all going to come crashing down and I'll be left without a baby again."

"There are definitely a lot of things that could go wrong, but it could also go right. You could carry this baby and be a mother just like you've always wanted."

I shook my head, more tears staining my already wet cheeks.

"I can't risk hoping for that."

He nodded like he understood and pulled me into another hug.

That night I slept in Devon's arms and in the morning he reluctantly agreed to my plan.

I didn't want to talk about the pregnancy.

Until my obstetrician could confirm it and tell me it was a healthy pregnancy, I didn't want to spend my time planning on a baby. I wanted to live our lives as normally as we could, and tell no one about the pregnancy. The fewer people who knew, the fewer people we'd have to tell when we inevitably lost the baby.

In one afternoon, that doctor had dangled the one thing I'd ever really wanted in front of me, and I couldn't be so reckless as just to grab hold and hang on. I wouldn't let myself be hurt that way again. I couldn't survive that kind of devastation.

Devon didn't like the plan, but he agreed, only if I agreed to some of his stipulations. In order for him to go along with my plan, I had to move in with him. He said he wanted me there every day and every night. I didn't have to officially move out of my apartment, but he wanted me to bring enough clothes over so I didn't have to go there every day, and he wanted us to live as a normal couple would.

I pretended as though I was a little put out by his request, but really, spending all my time with Devon, Ruby, and Jaxy was the best distraction. At least when I was around them I could pretend my mind wasn't always on the child I wished for so desperately.

Even with my previous history, the obstetrician wouldn't see me before I hit eight weeks. I tried to negotiate for an earlier appointment, but the scheduling nurse said it wouldn't make a difference. If we wanted proof of a viable pregnancy, we'd have to wait for the eight-week scan—that's when we'd be able to see the heartbeat.

Six weeks.

Six weeks of waiting for that appointment.

Six weeks that felt more like six years.

But Devon did exactly what I asked of him; he never mentioned the pregnancy or the baby.

At four weeks when my period never came, he was silent.

At five weeks when I went back to school and came home exhausted every day, napping and going to bed early, he said nothing.

At six weeks when I started vomiting every morning, he simply held my hair up and rubbed my back, saying not one word.

At seven weeks when I could no longer stand the smell of meat being grilled, I watched him smile, but he still said nothing.

At eight weeks when the doctor pointed to our baby on the screen, showing us the little fluttering of its heart, he finally leaned down and whispered in my ear, "You're having my baby."

Epilogue

Devon

Three Months Later

Spending Christmas in Hawaii was both good and bad. Good because, what's not good about Hawaii in December? But bad because for every Christmas until the end of time I'd be thinking about that one glorious holiday we spent in paradise.

Evie and Nate's wedding was wonderful, and I'll never forget how beautiful and grown-up Ruby looked standing next to Evie acting as her maid of honor. They opted to stay in Hawaii for their honeymoon, but since they were newlyweds, we hadn't seen much of them.

We planned on staying a week after the wedding and rented a condo right on the beach. It was my favorite time of day in Hawaii—sunset. And my favorite sunsets were the ones that included Grace. As I stood on the balcony of our rental, I could see Grace walking along the sand, Ruby and Jax walking alongside her, dress blowing in the wind, and baby bump on full display.

We'd decided to leave the sex of the baby a surprise, so I didn't know if she was carrying my son or my daughter; all I knew for sure was that it didn't matter in the slightest. She was healthy, the baby was healthy, my family was stitched together in the most beautiful way, and Grace was the thread that held us all together.

I think I knew from the moment I saw Grace and Jax under the shade of that tree that she'd be mine forever, but life and all its tangled webs made sure our path was just rocky enough to prove to Grace that I wasn't going anywhere, that there was nowhere else I'd rather be than with her, Ruby, Jax, and our new baby.

We'd waited until we hit twelve weeks to tell anyone about the pregnancy for two reasons: one, because we wanted to hit that safe zone, and two, because we wanted a little bit of time to acclimate. Those weeks – between eight and twelve – where I was the only one who knew Grace was carrying my baby— and was allowed to speak to her about it—were some of the best weeks of my life. I'd catch just a glimpse of her face and see the glow she had and know it was because she was pregnant with my baby. The first time she got out of the shower and I could see the tiniest of bumps, nothing was going to stop me from kneeling down right in front of her and running my hands, lips, and nose along the gentle slope.

None of her doctors could explain how it happened; most just called it a happy occurrence. And it was. But it was more than that. Our baby was a miracle. And if it could happen once, it could happen again. I never brought up another baby with Grace because I knew she wouldn't like it—she wanted to focus on reality, not fantasy—but I couldn't help but wonder if there were more babies in our future. I wanted to give her everything, and I knew she'd want another.

When we'd finally found the courage to tell Ruby and Jax they would have a little brother or sister, well, I'd never seen my kids so happy before.

Everything was absolutely perfect.

Except for one thing.

"Hey, you," Grace said as she slowly climbed the private stairs to our condo. "What are you doing out here all alone?"

"Enjoying the view," I said, pulling her close as she made it to the top of the stairs. My hand automatically found the part of her belly that stuck out the farthest and caressed her there. "How are you feeling?"

"Pregnant," she said with a smile. She never complained. Not once. And I understood that, knew that she viewed her pregnancy as a miracle and wasn't about to complain about something she'd wished for for so long. But I knew it took its toll on her. I'd have to be blind not to see the times she rubbed her back, or winced as she ran a hand over her belly.

"I have something for you," I said, gently taking her hand and leading her along the railing of the balcony.

"You do?"

"Yeah, down there." I dropped her hand and pointed to the black velvet box sitting atop the railing a few yards away. She stopped and I heard a quick intake of breath. Her face turned toward me, shock and surprise written all over it. "Go. Open it."

She walked slowly toward the box and when she reached it, her hand shook as she picked it up. I watched as she opened it slowly and waited, wanting desperately to see the reaction paint across her face. Grace never disappointed me, and I smiled as I watched her face go from surprise, to shock, and then straight to the ugly cry. She did that a lot too, now that she was carrying my baby, and I loved it. Almost as much as I loved her.

Her hand was covering her mouth, the tears were streaming down her cheeks, and she didn't notice when I went down to one knee just to the side of her.

"Babe?" I asked with a laugh. She turned to find me on my knee and started crying harder. "Ah, don't cry, Grace." I took her hand and pulled her to sit on my knee, the ring box still cradled in her shaking fingers. "I want us to be a family, Grace. All five of us. I met you and was captured by your compassion, and years later your heart's capacity still astounds me. If you let me, I'll spend the rest of my life trying to match it. I'll love you every day with everything I have, but it will still pale in comparison to the love you've shown me and my kids. Marry me, Grace? Let me love you forever."

"Are Ruby and Jax all right with this?" she asked, placing one trembling hand on my cheek, making me love her that much more.

"They helped me pick out the ring."

"You've given me everything I never thought I'd have."

"Then say yes, sweetheart." I brought her hand from my cheek to kiss her palm, watching her melt at my words.

"Yes," she whispered, then laughed as she threw her arms around my neck.

Ruby and Jax ran up the stairs giggling and laughing, hugging Grace as she slipped the ring on her finger. I had my whole world right in front of me, and everything was beautiful in the presence of Grace.

The End

Books by Anie Michaels

The Never Series

Never Close Enough

Never Far Away

Never Giving Up

Never Standing Still

Never Tied Down

The Love and Loss Series

The Absence of Olivia

The Presence of Grace

The Private Serials

Private Affairs

Private Encounters

Private Getaway

Private Property

Stand Alone Novels

The Space Between Us

Instead of You

To get updates about new releases, sales, and events, sign up for my monthly newsletter here.

Please feel free to follow me on all media platforms!

Facebook

Twitter

Instagram

Join my Facebook group for readers here.

Acknowledgements

Thank you to all the ladies in my awesome teamster group on Facebook. They tolerate a lot of random posts from me, along with a lot of insecurity and indecision. Thanks for always listening and offering your input and support. I love you all.

To my beta readers – Joanne Anderton, Michelle Tikal, Danielle Renee, Ali Crawely, Andrea TerKeurst, and Becca Dawn. Your insights were incredibly helpful and imperative to the final outcome of this book. Thank you for waiting all summer for my productivity to return, and for volunteering to read so readily, even though I left you without an ending. To Kelly Vaugh Morin, Andrea Luna Galante, and Stephanie Pace – Thank you for being my eagle eyes and helping me make the final product as close to perfect as I can manage. I am so grateful for your help.

To my family, thank you for supporting me and making this job a possibility. Especially to my husband who provides so much coffee which fuels my words.

To the readers – Thank you for giving Devon a chance. I know he might not have started as your favorite, but I love him because he's flawed. He needed a happy ending and I am glad I could give it to him. I hope you'll continue to enjoy the series as it grows.

Thank you, Olivia Ventura, for your work on this novel, and to everyone at Hot Tree Editing for always fitting me in and providing a superior experience.

Special thanks to AJ Harmon for being my favorite cheerleader and always supporting me. I want to be you when I grow up.